A Mad Bent Diva

A Mad Bent Diva

a collection of life affirming death threats, vignettes, and epithets

David Bateman

First Edition

Hidden Brook Press
www.HiddenBrookPress.com
writers@HiddenBrookPress.com

A Mad Bent Diva:

a collection of life affirming death threats, vignettes, and epithets

by David Bateman

Editor – Raymond Helkio

Cover Photograph – David Bateman

Cover Design – Richard M. Grove

Layout and Design – Richard M. Grove

Typeset in Garamond

Printed and bound in Canada

Distributed in USA by Ingram,

in Canada by Hidden Brook Distribution

Library and Archives Canada Cataloguing in Publication

Bateman, David, 1956-, author
        A mad bent diva : a collection of life affirming death threats, vignettes, and epithets / David Bateman. -- First edition.

Short stories.
ISBN 978-1-927725-37-5 (softcover)

        I. Title.

PS8553.A8254M33 2017   C813'.54   C2017-900482-4

CONTENTS

suicide notes...
a collection of life affirming death threats,
vignettes, and epithets

Foreword
by Raymond Helkio

Decidedly Bent

The first time I met David was during his performance at Videofag (Toronto). Dressed as a fairy, he came out on roller skates. And then things got really bent. Since then we've collaborated on short films, plays, performances, and musical musings, all queer. Being queer is what makes us different, and it's only through our differences that we can celebrate who we are. We each experience the world through a filter that is unique to us and these experiences can teach others about themselves as it can comfort those it resonates with.

A Mad Pansy In Search Of A Father Figure Named Jesus

Magical, poignant, and sometimes heart-wrenching, *A Mad Bent Diva* is a reference to David's life. Is he mad as in crazy, or is he angry and bitter? The answer is both, and it depends on what stage of his life you are reading about. Sure, David may tell you that some of these stories are not about him, but they are. A writer cannot separate themselves from the text like a gay boy cannot detangle a mother's metaphorical umbilical cord that, in complex ways, filled with love and misunderstanding, simultaneously binds, gags, liberates, and empowers. As David reveals in *Roberta*, "The sudden loss of my own mother made me acutely aware of how time never stands still long enough for all good things to come full circle between loved ones before we have to say goodbye."

My Mother's Purse is about a boy rummaging through his mother's purse in search of answers of his own. An unnamed entity posing the question, "Is that your man-purse?" A demeaning, homophobic and mean-spirited comment intended to shame and humiliate. David's retort, only the second line in this story, is his unapologetic response followed by his unique brand of dry wit. "Yes. Are those your man boobs?"

In *Trickster White (a monologue)*, David as an adult finds himself in a one-sided relationship with a macho man who can't see beyond himself. And so what would a self-respecting queen do in a situation like this? Instead of changing the situation, he reinvents how he sees the relationship. One minute he has a disconnected boyfriend, the next he's signing his name as Elizabeth Taylor and likening his lover to Jesus. Love, or this "unbearable non-regrettable lightness of being" – as David refers to it - is the cathartic space between our hopes, dreams and the reality that surrounds us.

On Being A Diva
The next time I met David we were outside of a coffee shop off Church Street. It was to be our first day of filming for *Hamlet In A Hot Tub* in Spa XS, a bathhouse in downtown Toronto. I walked up to the shop with my gear, David is sitting outside on a bench, legs pressed together. He's wearing a black cap with a large brim and large Jackie O sunglasses. I walk up to him, say good morning, he shifts both legs towards me, his makeup shimmering in the early morning sun. Without missing a beat, he peers over his glasses and announces "Mr. DeMille, I am ready for my close-up now."

Like David, A Mad Bent Diva is a magical world of curiosities and chaos fuelled by will-ful innocence. This collection of works is like riding the Swan ride at an amusement park, only to realize it's morphed into a spinning teacup on a rollercoaster, all the while your mother blows kisses at you from below. This is what I imagine his childhood to have been like. A twisted queer day at the amusement park with an omnipresent, complicated mother at the helm of the spinning teacup and the gliding swan.

In these pages are works of fiction, creative non-fiction, poetry and prose. Performance, spoken word, and song. David's voice rings through every character, ever so bent, always true. This collection is as much about him as it is about you. We are all mad, bent and are capable of diva-like behaviour but David, well, she is the real thing. She's Liza Minnelli inside a Bitch Diva,* she's got the audience wrapped around her diamond ringed finger, she's a diva, a princess and an original sin.

Bitch Diva is an acclaimed & infamous Toronto based singer who performs, in drag - everything from pop tunes to jazz standards, arias and Broadway songs. Aka as Michael Fitzgerald, Bitch Diva has generously shared the stage with David Bateman on numerous occasions over the past few decades.

Tampax Tale

Tampax was always something tucked into a paper bag that my mother folded, slid into my pants pocket, early nineteen-sixties, and said, "Give this to the cashier, Sweetheart, then tell her to read the note inside, but don't look at it yourself, and don't open the bag once she has filled it for you." I don't know if my mother ever figured out that I can't keep secrets—and when someone tells me not to do something, I just do it.

It was a short walk from our house to the Pharmacy in the strip mall by the bowling alley, past the barber shop, with glimpses of those hot Italian barbers, the Atlas brothers, with their beautiful hairy necks, sometimes shaven clean sometimes rippled with feathery waves of thin, heavenly grasses over the edge of their white barber collars, like slender black reeds on taut marshy seas of flesh, like an acre of night in the eyes of a curious child exploring heaven's cellar, like a forest of poetry etched and swaying at the nape

> *against dew, dark skin*
> *sweet swarthy sexy haiku*
> *braying boyish lust.*

Hushed by my timid manner, I saw their necks like I saw Tampax, sites of desire I didn't understand yet lurking in secret spaces I was trusted with. They would cut my hair, sit me high on a flat-bottomed wooden hobbyhorse that didn't rock, lifting my little seven-year-old frame toward their manly scissors.

One day I was told to fill my mother's secret Tampax order after my haircut was done. Phil Atlas raised me high out of the hobbyhorse's saddle. I pulled the money out of my pocket, and the folded paper bag fell on the floor, the word scribbled on the little square of paper. Phil Atlas bent over and picked it up and said, "What ya got in there, little fella?"

I looked at the word and silently moved my lips to the shape of those unlikely syllables: tam-pax. Through the eyes and the larynx of a syllabically challenged child, Tampax made me think of Ajax, a little town near where I lived, and I also knew that it was the name of a cleaning product named after a Greek hero. I wanted to sound smart and confident in front of that sexy barber, so I said, "It's Tampax for my mom. I get it for her all the time. I think it comes from Ajax named after a handsome Greek man." The three other barbers and their patrons all looked up, startled, uncomfortable, and laughing. I was a timid child, blonde and small, and no match for all the testosterone assembled in that barbershop that day. Phil Atlas had always lifted me into the hobbyhorse harness, but this day was a turning point. I was getting a little big for the lift, and from that day on he let me get in and out all by myself, and he wasn't as friendly as he had always been. My mother also noticed that he wasn't friendly to her anymore, and didn't comment on her nice new hotpants outfits like he used to when she first became a widow.

My mother always looked so fresh and lovely in those gauzy translucent shorts and matching top, all in yellow and white with soft patches of shadowy grey. I grew up fascinated with my mother's body, her fashion choices, and men's hairy necks and how sleek and lovely they looked when they trimmed the hair at the crest of their shoulders, and my father's hairless chest was always a map of the world for me on Sunday mornings. Crawling into bed with my parents and peering over the sleek, exposed mounds of his upper torso, enchanted by geography I had yet to navigate and conquer. And the lacy edges of my mother's aquamarine night gown, frill and brawn inhabiting my little head, like myth and story at such a tender age—like Greek Gods and the young men and older women who must have loved them. I think it all just made me want to have sex with men named Ajax, and women with secret folded notes, in barber shops filled with laughter aimed at childish mythological stories about Tampax, and memories of how my mother bathed me with her when I was small enough to fit in the same bathtub. Her perfect breasts were like those shaved necks to me. It all just meshed together with thoughts of beautiful Italian barbers glaring at me as my waifish body grew out of equine child seats, but never growing into manhood until I was middle-aged. Forever that little boy, sent on his own to play with adults, but never given proper instructions, just notes folded into flattened paper bags, and men who could never love me the way I dreamed Greek heroes would.

Sometimes it only gets better when we unfold those notes ourselves, and refuse to keep secrets, and do what we're told not to, and learn to love women bathing us like goddesses—half afraid but terribly curious, in a Greek tragedy kind of way, of what we might find within the luscious, folded layers of all these mytho-logical bodies.

Incidentally

Martin and Dennis were sitting in the kitchen, drinking tea and eating toast, chatting about the latest incident. Martin began to explain how he felt.

> MARTIN: It was embarrassing. I felt very lonely, and a bit ridiculous. And I've never really felt loneliness before, not like that. Up until now it has always been solitude, never loneliness.

Dennis concealed his light laughter, and whispered.

> DENNIS: It happens to everyone. Don't worry about it.

Martin was not at all comforted by his words—and despite his closest friend's effort to conceal his mirth, he could tell that Dennis found it all very amusing. Martin tried to ignore him as he continued to explain what had upset him so much.

> MARTIN: I can't stop thinking about how sad it looked, just lying there on the floor, all soft and broken. It was humiliating. It was like a little bird, a little dead bird.

As he spoke he looked closely at the lines on Dennis's face, and reached over to touch one of them, his favourite one, just like the old days when they were much younger lovers and physical affection was something they shared more frequently. It was the line just above the bridge of Dennis's nose, the first one Martin had noticed over a decade ago. It was deeper now, and cut across otherwise taut flesh like a tiny ravine—no longer a sleek thoroughfare running seamlessly between his beautiful eyebrows, framing the upper tip of his long, perfectly shaped, oddly aquiline proboscis. What was once a pristine causeway of taut flesh was now a bridge over troubled waters, so to speak. Dennis's face was a map and Martin, despite their closeness, was a tourist returning to a beloved site one too many times.

Dennis gently took Martin's hand from his own brow and kissed it as he launched into one of his very predictable bouts of half-hearted encouragement.

> DENNIS: My dear, dear friend. You have so much to live for. Try not to let these little things bother you. Let's just get ready for our obligatory weekend adventure and put the memory of soft broken things behind us. They're incidental, just props filling our lives with material clutter. Forget them.

But Martin couldn't. It was a living thing, almost—an egg splattered on the kitchen floor. And every living thing bothered him, even inanimate objects like plates and forks and glasses and knives. They lived in his memory. He felt trapped in a tiny, cluttered apartment, and there were times, when he was out doing daily errands, that he was afraid to go home. It had all become too familiar and reliable, and it was getting on his nerves. He would fidget and moan, all by himself, about the smallest occurrences. Nothing seemed to work out the way he wanted it to, and when he dropped his breakfast on the floor that morning, all alone in his one-bedroom apartment, it just seemed so sad. The decorative plate with the whiskey-sour recipe on it had broken into four perfect pieces, like a pie, and the eggs were soft and runny on the worn-out parquet floor, and the Anne Boleyn eggcup that he bought in the gift shop at the Tower of London was smashed. Her head was all over the place. At the last minute he had decided to scramble the egg instead of hard boil it, but the eggcup was already set out on the tray—and it looked so lovely beside the whiskey-sour cocktail snack plate. So he left the eggcup sitting there, empty and waiting to be beheaded once again without even a hardboiled egg to show for its trouble. Martin relied on the order of all the objects in his life, and he needed to be able to explain to Dennis how it made him feel when it all fell apart, even though he knew his oldest friend would never take it seriously.

MARTIN: You've said it yourself, Dennis. You know you have. Food, people handling and eating food, there is something very vulnerable and sad in that. We can dress ourselves up and go out to dinner and eat slowly and carefully, and appear to be in complete control of everything around us—the knives and the forks, the spoons and the wine goblets, the perfectly laundered white napkins. But underneath it all there is such a humiliating fragility, and when something unexpected and catastrophic does occur, and the food flies, well, there is nothing sadder than the look on people's faces. One minute they are enjoying a meal and the next minute they are helpless and the menu is all over the bloody place, and more often than not, all over them, and that's the worst of it—on their clothes and their arms and, God forbid, all over their faces. And that is how I felt this morning, and I need you to take it seriously. I know there are more important things to consider in life, but it was my last free-range egg and my last garlic poppy seed bagel and my last packet of ketchup stolen from the IHOP, and I love those matching cocktail recipe plates, and now one is gone forever, and I just wanted to enjoy my breakfast on my own before I embarked on this annual, ill-conceived weekend at the godforsaken beach with a bunch of close friends I've grown to barely tolerate. Couldn't you have just gently consoled me and left it at that, instead of giving me some prosaic little bit of fluff about the memory of soft broken things? You are such a fucking poet sometimes.

Dennis laughed out loud and made no attempt whatsoever to ameliorate his friend's anxiety and mild disgust. He responded with his typically insensitive candour.

DENNIS: You are such a diva, a mad bent diva. And you call me the poet! Now cut the crap and get ready or I'm out of here.

Martin left the room, concealing his tears. About an hour later Dennis left by himself. Martin was nowhere to be found in the tiny apartment. Flighty queen that he was made out to be, he must have quietly flown the coop. Funny, Dennis didn't hear the door close. He just thought Martin had gone into his bedroom to pack a few more things. He looked in all the rooms, through the glass on the balcony door, and then he sat in the kitchen, finished his tea, and waited for half an hour, and when nothing happened he looked around again and realized his friend was really gone. Then he heard some shouting on the street ten floors below, and he got up and left, without Martin.

* * *

DENNIS: You should have seen the look on his face. It was heartbreaking. But I couldn't take it seriously. It was a goddamn egg on a bagel and a tacky plate and he made such a fuss about it, and I suppose the ketchup looked like blood, and I was actually relieved to finally see that ridiculous eggcup destroyed. He was obsessed with it. And the plate broke—it was uncanny—broken in four perfect pieces, like a pie. I'm sure he'll call soon and one of us can drive all the way back into the city to get him. He is such a diva sometimes. But I wish he were here right now. Dinner conversation is never as much fun without him.

Dennis had left Martin's building by the side door, closer to where he had parked his car, so he had no idea what the ruckus was all about out front. It was probably some vagrant having a full frontal fit on the sidewalk. He didn't approve of the way Martin always stopped and chatted with them, gave them whatever change he had in his pockets, sometimes even bills. Martin never seemed in the least put out by their presence and their scavenging ways. Dennis, on the other hand, resented what he considered an invasion of his public space, and he did not feel any sympathy for the down-and-out.

DENNIS: If people have not managed their affairs properly, then they deserve to suffer.

When Dennis had said this to Martin, the week before the egg and bagel incident, it had served as a liberating missive that Martin would take note of and then refuse to forget for quite some time. Instead of paying Dennis back for the hundred-dollar loan to get his phone reconnected, he freed himself from the drudgery of making good on a minor debt to someone who didn't need the money urgently. Instead, he sent the cash to a friend who was having a difficult time making ends meet. She had lost fingers to a crippling form of arthritis and needed extra money in her hands right away, so she got it and Dennis didn't. It seemed to make sense as far as Martin was concerned, and it made him feel like a contemporary Robin Hood.

Dennis was by no means rich, just a little comfortable, for the time being. Martin, Dennis, and all their close friends were in for a challenging future as gay old men without an excess of resources and no savings to speak of. For now all they could do was go on living and enjoying whatever they could manage: a weekend at the beach in a rented cabin big enough for five, but shared by the seven of them. Of course, there were the two little tents for the brothers, and it would be a mad, lovely, midsummer treat they could ill afford. But now, what with Martin's disappearing act, there were only six, and they spent a good deal of time lamenting his absence. Kevin was the first one to speak up.

> KEVIN: Dennis, you dickhead! Why the hell did you leave him there in the first place?

Dennis tried to defend himself but felt sheepish and sad.

> DENNIS: I couldn't find him. One minute he's in the kitchen drinking tea and eating toast with me, and the next minute he's gone. I didn't hear the door close. He must have just slipped out, quietly, like he does.

Kevin knew they must have been fighting about something. They always did.

> KEVIN: Well you shouldn't have argued with him. We all came here for him, and now he's not even here, and it's your fucking fault. Asshole!

Dennis wiped a single tear from his eye and gulped back the rest of his hefty gin and tonic, with a thin slice of cucumber floating mindlessly midway between four pristine chunks of penis-shaped ice.

DENNIS: He'll show up. Trust me. He always does, at the most unexpected moments, and I wish you'd stop bringing that ice cube tray shaped like cocks. I hate them. They were fun about twenty years ago. Now they're just tacky and stupid.

Kevin laughed as he took a dripping dick-shaped cube from his glass and threw it across the room at Dennis. It landed in the fireplace and sizzled lightly before dying a smouldering death. Ice cubes never smoulder but it was such fun imagining that they did.

Maev threw her arms in the air and laughed and laughed as she told the two of them to shut the fuck up.

MAEV: Drink up boys. We're having a bonfire soon, and you two are cut off. One hot dog each and a couple of marshmallows and then you're both driving into the goddamn city and finding him and bringing him here.

They knew there was no point in arguing. She always got her way, Maev did. And who had a name like that anyway? They were all such inbred waspy creatures. A woman in their midst, with a mind of her own and the body of an Amazonian huntress—tits the size of perfectly formed flotation devices. Maev was a welcome distraction from their whiny ways. Kevin often remarked that they all objectified her and took her for granted. All she had to say to that was, "Well, Sport, men always take me for granted. At least when they're gay, I can objectify them too and feel really good about it. You're all gorgeous and funny and bitchy and kind, and I just love being around you." And then she would kiss Kevin, long and sensuously, and thanked God for bisexuality.

They all knew that the two of them, Kevin and Maev, screwed a few times over the course of their annual summer beach weekend, but no one said a word, except for the odd remark over dinner and the obvious misogynist food metaphors, but that was another matter entirely, one which Maev always took complete control: "You're a bunch of pussies, but at least I've got one. Keep your clams shut while Kevin fills mine!" They were all a little jealous of Kevin, even though they had their reservations about what they mistook for his decidedly undecided sexuality. Maev's sexual politics were more advanced than the gaggle of gay men she socialized with. She often wondered if they had any clear political bent, and gave them no slack when it came to any clichéd tendencies toward a mistrust of bisexual bravado.

> MAEV: You're all just jealous because your precious little dicks only move in one direction, and boys, I have no problem with that. But when one of you decides to point their divining rod toward my fountain of youth then don't be a fucking ponce-de-moron and try to steal him away from me. I won't play the little complacent fag hag and sit around admiring your fading beauty and pine for a fairy of my own. Fag Hag! It's one of the ugliest little rhymes in the whole gay god-damn world! Sex is a plane, a geometric fucking plane, it refracts in every which way, and it's loose, and when it lands face down in my luscious lap don't fuck with me or you'll have one irate goddess to deal with.

Kevin admired the way she would light into his closest friends, and felt proud that she chose him out of all of them—that they chose each other for their intense, casual encounters. He was like her. He knew what he wanted, and got it whenever he put his mind to it. In the midst of Maev's rant and their collective laughter Dennis grabbed the gin bottle from the rolling booze table and exclaimed, his babyish bravado trying to hide the fact that he did feel guilty for leaving Martin behind.

DENNIS: Fine, we'll go get him, while you all lounge around here sucking each other's cocks. But not before sunset. I'm not missing a single goddamn sunset for anyone. And I wouldn't mind a blowjob, one for the road, in place of my second gin and tonic. Anybody handy?

They all just laughed but knew that Kevin would give him one in the driver's seat, on the straight and narrow of an empty highway, before they hit the city streets. Maev knew—everyone knew. The orgiastic nature of their seasonal festivities; it was like musical chairs. It was just one of those things—those funny things, as Cole Porter said, that flew in their windows wide, made them happy, then flew out again. What was this thing? They all knew exactly what it was, among them, thriving even in middle age. It was love. And the sunset was just such a breathtaking cliché as the six of them sat in the sand, bordering the edge of the front lawn and just stared in silence until Greg broke the perfect stillness with his raffish bark.

GREG: Will ya look at that, eh? It's bee-you-tee-full. Our Nana always said it like that, *bee-yoo-tee-full*, whether she was talking about a great view or a bite of apple pie. We would take her to a smorgasbord, she always pronounced it *smogasborg*, and she'd try one of every dessert, would put them all on the same damn plate, then sit down at the table in the restaurant and pick away at them all, one at a time, until they were gone, like she was devouring the finest delicacies on earth, and it was usually just a bunch of green Jello cubes, and a tart, and a dried-up piece of cake.

Billy dove right into the middle of Greg's monologue, like he always did.

BILLY: You're exaggerating you crazy old fuck. I was there.

Our Nana was the sweetest woman on earth and those desserts were delicacies to her, and they weren't dried-up. She enjoyed them all. Don't make fun of her. And by the way, she hated Jello.

Greg barked back at his brother.

GREG: She fuckin' loved Jello. Lime Jello! And I'm not making fun. I love that memory. We don't have the same fuckin' memory, okay? Have yours, bitch, and I'll have mine, for Christ's sake, and Martin reminds me so much of her, of Nana.

Billy rolled his eyes and scowled at Greg.

BILLY: A middle-aged queen, the gayest man on earth, reminds you of our grandmother? I've heard everything from you, but this takes the cake.

GREG: Martin loves objects just like Nana did. Remember how she glued that lamp back together, the one that sat between our beds, after you kicked it off the night table while you were jerkin' off and broke it into a dozen pieces, and she cried the whole time she was doing it. That's how Martin must have felt when he dropped his breakfast and everything smashed.

BILLY: What the fuck are you talking about? You kicked the goddamn lamp off the night table, not me.

Maev intervened and put a stop to their sibling antics.

MAEV: Oh you two just be quiet. Brothers in love. Fuck. You squabble like an old married couple. Enjoy the goddamn sunset. Stick one of those ice cubes up your twin assholes and chill out, bitches!

BILLY & GREG: We are not twins. We're three years apart.
I would never share a womb with him. He's too selfish.

No one even noticed which one of them had spoken. They were all too enamoured by the last ribbon of light as it dipped below the cloud and resonated in pale mauve highlights along the edge of the lake's blurred horizon. Voices mingled as they mirrored each other in a mélange of alliterative mutterings. Who knew who was talking? Who cared?

"It's scarlet, not mauve, you mincing moron. A scarlet ribbon!"

"Look closely at the edges you moody queen. They're mauve, the way they merge with those magnificent strips of cloud that frame the menacing sky."

It wasn't a full sunset because of the narrow clouds hanging low against the edge of the water, but it was just as beautiful, with the remnants of the sun giving the top edge of the clouds a piercing outline, like a line of flames sinking into the west. Gary was the quietest of them all, and no one noticed when he took snapshots of those final moments—the laughing faces, the loving, argumentative glances, the bee-yoo-tee-full incomplete sunset and the barely defined horizon. With a cheap digital camera, blighted by sand caught in the lens, Gary managed to capture those sentimental, grainy moments just before the orange became a soft yellow with hazy shafts of light shooting upward and making him feel silly because beautiful sunsets made Gary think of heaven, and he didn't believe in heaven. But he liked to take pictures that reminded him of the things he couldn't quite grasp—or even begin to imagine being possible.

* * *

No one knew who started the fire, just after midnight. It burned through the middle of the wooden steps to the empty cabin just beyond the edge of their rented property. They were all afraid they would have to pay for it. The bonfire had been put out. Sparks would never have flown that far from the beach—everyone was a little drunk—and Dennis and Kevin had already left for the city to find Martin a full hour before the flames began. Luckily Billy caught it quickly and had it out with a small red extinguisher within minutes. But it caused quite a stir among other late night partiers who ran screaming from their own little patch of beach to the rental office to disclose their fear that someone's cabin was burning to the ground. It could have been so much worse. They all awoke to the shouts of the rental manager's wife, banging on the front door of their cabin and demanding to be let in. "I want you all out of here!"

It had just been a tiny illegal bonfire. They shielded it with their beach umbrellas and only let it blaze for less than half an hour, long enough for a few marshmallows each and a couple of campfire ditties, and then they put it out. But it was enough to make everyone think they had started the one at the nearby cabin.

And then there was Billy, sitting among them, shrieking in his out of tune bass to his favourite festive lyric—a lyric that he felt defined this group of people that he loved so much, and was spending another harrowing weekend with.

> *Sing around the campfire!*
> *Join the Camp Fire Girls.*
> *Join the laughter, join the fun,*
> *It's a wonderful time for everyone.*
> *It's a busy day, and when... it's... done....*
>
> *What fun to sing around the campfire!*
> *'Neath the moon above,*
> *Sing "wohelo", sing "wohelo",*
> *Work – Health – Love!*

Sitting together, in a row, they all looked similar, and from a distance, even close up, one could easily mistake one for the other, like brothers. Even Maev could have passed for the lone renegade sister in this unrelated family of mostly male members. They were a gallery of attractive gay white males who were trying to go with the ebb and flow of diverse queer history. But they frequently lapsed into a kind of GQ gloss-over of matching cashmere sweater proportions—draped over their shoulders, like manly shawls, sleeves folded neatly in a V just below the Adam's apple, with Maev in their midst wearing a tie-dyed sarong and an aquamarine mohair cardigan.

Billy did get a couple of bizarre photos of the little porch on fire just before he doused it. He borrowed Gary's little digital just after they finished making out, grinding against the side of a tree, on their way to bed. They always flirted but never fucked. Gary headed straight to his room while Billy lingered outdoors.

BILLY: I just want to take a few shots of the moon. Please.

He hated loaning his camera, but he couldn't say no to Billy. As he fell asleep Gary smiled at the memory of those loud, slightly lyrical, throaty, ghoulish sounds, made even more bizarre by Billy's wavering low voice, making a decidedly butch/femme plea for membership in their bizarre little clan as he sang, *"Sing around the campfire! Join the campfire girls!"*

Yes, indeed, that loud little ditty might have tipped the other guests off about the fire and sent them running to the rental office with false ammunition. It was a smouldering matchstick that one of the secretive lovers dropped as they left the empty cabin—lighting a cigarette and carelessly letting the hot match fall under the steps as he quietly made his exit with his two unlikely bedfellows in tow.

* * *

When Dennis and Kevin got back to the lake without Martin, too distracted to check their cell phones for any texts, they were already frantic. The empty cabin, and the absence of their friends, was just too much for them to take in. The manager heard them shouting at each other at around 3:00 a.m. and came running over to their cabin, still anxious over the fire and his wife's rage about these loud, negligent summer vacationers he always gave a discount, for what appeared to be no good reason at all.

> CABIN MANAGER: Your friends are gone, to the Bluewater Motel, just down the road. Tell them I'm sorry: it wasn't their fault. I figured it out. There was a little fire. Don't ask. Trust me. I won't charge you the rental fee. Now get out of here. I've had enough summer-fun bullshit for one night.

Kevin was crying by this time, and the manager felt bad that his wife had unwittingly put the blame in the wrong place. He looked embarrassed, and very recent memories filled his heart and his crotch.

> CABIN MANAGER: Okay, get them. Bring them back here. I'll give you the weekend free, and next summer too. Okay? Sorry for the screw-up, guys.

Dennis put his arm on Kevin's shoulder, thanked the manager, and tried to comfort his friend.

> DENNIS: I'll call Billy on his cell. We won't have to go there. They'll come back, and we can tell them then. I hope he has his cell turned on. And thanks for the blowjobs. They made the drive less boring. You're swell!

The whole gang, they were back within twenty minutes. The front room lights in the cabin were all on as they straggled in, still a little drunk and very tired. Maev was the first to speak.

> MAEV: Well, this weekend is really turning out well. Where's Martin?

Kevin was trying to suppress his grief, but Maev's beautiful, husky voice always made him emotional at the best of times. He just started sobbing. Greg rushed over to comfort Kevin.

> GREG: What the fuck's going on? Where is he? What's happened? Is he okay?

If there had been a staircase in the cabin it would have made Martin's appearance so much more thrilling. Like Norma Desmond's in the musical version of Sunset Boulevard. But there was no staircase, just a little wooden door to one of the bedrooms.

> MARTIN: I'm fine. But I seem to be the one who always gets called the diva. You bunch of mad bent depraved queens. What on earth are you going on about? Me, my robe, all of my fashionable luggage, and my vintage picnic basket that I lugged here on a filthy Greyhound—it was disgusting—we are all perfectly fine, and we're thrilled to finally be here among all you glorious assholes.

Martin had come out of the small room in his underwear, dragging a satin robe behind him, looking very thin, yet elegant, just at that stage where one looks like they've lost a bit of weight, before the gaunt unhealthy period threatens to set in. But he would bounce back. He always did, so far. Dennis's first impulse, when he saw Martin, was anger.

> DENNIS: We thought you were dead, you prick. Where the fuck were you when I left the co-op?

> MARTIN: I was on the balcony, Shithead.

> DENNIS: You were not. I looked there. You were gone.

> MARTIN: The roof balcony. I went to cut some basil to bring up here, and when I got back I figured you just threw one of your random fits and left without me. So I took the fucking bus. And there was a bit of a, well, ruckus, downstairs when I got back, and I couldn't rush out to find you. I was immersed in the trauma of it all. It was awful. But I am not going to talk about any of that. Let's salvage what's left of this little weekend fiasco.

Dennis's curiosity was piqued, because he had a faint memory of hearing something as he left the co-op.

> DENNIS: What ruckus? What the fuck happened?

Martin responded crisply, with a melancholy, irritated air about him.

> MARTIN: Someone jumped. Okay, are you happy now? Someone jumped from their fucking balcony in the middle of a hot summer afternoon and landed in the goddamn flowerbed. It was just bloody awful. And the poor victim was just so badly dressed, and I just know that the gardening

committee will be meeting right away to refurbish the bed. There, are you satisfied? I told you. And it's made me feel sick, and I'm going to bed.

DENNIS: They all made us, me and Kevin, go back to the city to find you, and when we got there some people were still up, sitting on the curb at the front of your place, drinking and chatting, some of them crying. We overheard them talking. We thought they meant you. They were talking about a suicide. They didn't even know the person. One of them thought it might be you, but he was high and had no idea where the body had been taken. So we just came back here, to break the news to everyone. Kevin wanted to check all the hospitals, but I couldn't stomach the thought.

MARTIN: Oh for Christ's sake. You bastard! You didn't even bother going to St. Michael's. It's two minutes from my place. And besides, you know I'm not suicidal. I took the depression test and scored very high on the non-depressive side, and I told all of you all about it at Bro'Bar last Friday. I just have very infrequent suicidal thoughts. That's normal. I've lived long enough, longer than I expected. My life has been thrilling. It's been just great, but I would just like it to end, while I am still moderately young, in about forty years, when I'm ninety. It may sound morbid to all of you, but really, I want it to end quietly, beautifully, like a movie, like a fucking sunset! But I'm sure as hell not going to make it end in some broken, bloody heap in a well-kept, immaculately-manicured flowerbed! The poor dear. Oh God. That's tacky, and way too glamorous for assholes like all of you to understand.

Dennis snapped back.

DENNIS: You were just so goddamn sad this morning, about dropping your breakfast on the floor.

MARTIN: Yes. I was, and you were no help, so I just left the apartment to take my mind off of your very predictable insensitivity and I picked a shit load of fresh basil, and put it in a cute little basket with a calico napkin from Home-Sense to line it. We can have it tomorrow with tomatoes and bocconcini. I hope someone brought balsamic and olive oil. I told someone to. I cannot, for the life of me, remember who.

Dennis hugged Martin and whispered in his ear.

DENNIS: I brought the oil and vinegar, sweetheart. It's all good.

MARTIN: Well then, perfect. Tomorrow I'm making omelettes with fresh salmon, Caesar salad, and cubed cantaloupe. We'll have a very late brunch, around five.

Between bouts of laughter, Maev was yawning. She interjected, as she kissed Martin on the cheek.

MAEV: Okay, boys, I'm off to bed. This has been a fabulous first evening. A fire, an unfashionable, misleading suicide, and the promise of a delicious late brunch, verging on dinner. Nothing can top this.

* * *

Topping the events that had already taken place would be difficult, but three secret lovers were trying to do just that. They had jumped up onto the little landing at the top of the burned, broken steps and scrambled back into the cabin. Naked on the soft sandy floorboards where their initial meeting had begun, and laughing softly, they all agreed it was time to turn on their signature song on the little CD player, very low, so no one would hear. Debby Boone sang out loud and clear, like the naughty zealot she was raised to be by her Hollywood-heartthrob daddy and her tongues-speaking Mama.

> *Rolling at sea, adrift on the waters.*
> *Could it be finally I'm turning for home?*
> *Finally, a chance to say, "Hey, I love you."*
> *Never again, to be all alone.*
> *It can't be wrong, when it feels so right.*
> *'Cause you, you light up my life.*

Their lips were full and damp, as their arms and legs became a triangular bacchanalian retreat from everything their lives expected of them. It wasn't unusual, when they were together, to find more than one member installed in a single orifice. The cabin was risky but they couldn't resist. They would just lock themselves in the back bedroom and let loose, quietly yet passionately. It had always been the same set of cabins, for ten summers now. Only two of them knew that the rates were much higher for other renters. They had started the tryst their first summer there, and it just never let up. Even as they grew older their lust never faltered. The cabin owner/manager would even come into the city, once or twice during the winter, to see them at Bro'Bar, and it would end in a posh hotel room nearby. It wasn't something he expected so late in life, but it was a thrilling respite from the comfort of the small, tourist town life he loved, but was a little bored with.

Even in their drunken summer reveries it was always safe, more romantic than sexual, more kind than kin. They knew each other's bodies, and fit together like a womb of forbidden comfort, and the oral and anal fissures that made their erotic affections complete were carefully and tenderly navigated with fingers, mouths, flavoured lubricant and durable condoms—lips and tongues so fully integrated into each other's bodies, it was hard to tell, at certain moments, who was who. Yes indeed, there was always a risk, but they had felt, from the very beginning, that is was worth the effortless effort. And after Martin's safe return—they saw him from their tents as he straggled in—no one cared who was absent when Dennis and Kevin returned and the whole misunderstanding was cleared up.

The secretive lovers always brought their own little tents and slept at the edge of the property. They just got out of the car after arriving from the motel and fled to their canvas solitudes. The lanterns in their tents alerted the stocky, sexy, hairy little rental manager. He slipped quietly out of bed, his wife of thirty years sound asleep beside him, to join the campy campers in the only unrented cabin on site, always set aside for their secret rendezvous. They didn't usually do it twice in a single night. He only hoped, after all the ruckus about the little fire, that this time he would not light a cigarette and drop the match carelessly under the broken steps once they had finished making love. Hopefully, the snapshots from Gary's cheap little borrowed digital wouldn't reveal the names embossed in gold on the matchbook from the bar that they owned together. A book of matches—the incidental material trappings of a successful family business. The taboos, the trade-offs, and the titillation. The beaches, the betrayals, and the bee-yoo-tee-full imperfect sunsets. They all had their perks—and their limitations. They were, in every sense of the word, 'incidentally' inclined. Like the sunsets they enjoyed together once a year, the surface was bright, glaring, and had an immaculate garish beauty that none of them could resist. But underneath the queer gloss there was a lyric, campy depth that even a French composer and two American lyricists could not have set to music in a more fitting manner—

> *The summer smiles the summer knows*
> *And unashamed, she sheds her clothes*
> *The summer smooths the restless sky*
> *And lovingly she warms the sand on which you lie...*
>
> *Twists the world round her summer finger*
> *Let's you see the wonder of it all...*

—Michel Legrand

Palindrome (for two Queens)

Q1: Lana Anal. It's my new drag name. Do you like it?

Q2: I prefer the one you were using last week.

Q1: What was it? I've forgotten already.

Q2: Ona Nyst.

Q1: Right. You have such a good memory. No one would have understood that one. Onanist is such an out-of-date term.

Q2: How about Miss Ogynist?

Q1: It's tacky, and offensive, and it's already been done, ages ago.

Q2: By who? And when? It's not like you need to be original. There's no such thing, sweetheart.

Q1: In *City of Night*, a drag queen introduces herself, in a bar in the French Quarter, to the protagonist as Miss Ogynist.

Q2: I loved it when you were in that all 'girl' country drag band, Victoria Haliburton and the Townships. You really had those Tammy Wynette numbers down. *Sometimes it Makes Me Hard to be a Woman* was my favourite.

Q1: Those were the days. And when Hannah would fly in and do a guest spot. Her version of *I Fall to Pieces* was so moving.

Q2: Right. It was hilarious. I'd almost forgotten. What did she call it?

Q1: It was not hilarious. It was touching and very poignant. She called it *I Call For Pizza. (sings) You ask me to act like we've never met, you ask me to forget, pretend we've never necked, but you walk by, I get high, and call for pizza…*

Q2: Yeah, she was great. Haven't seen her in ages.

Q1: She just called me last week, wants to come over and photograph Jolene.

Q2: Jolene?

Q1: You've forgotten her too? Misogynist! You forget all of the important women in my life.

Q2: Remind me. Who the fuck is Jolene?

Q1: The reindeer. How could you forget the reindeer? It was the first time you stuck that pencil thin digit of yours up my orange blossom special. After the show, right on the stage, with Jolene watching. We always sat her there. She was our mascot. I used to dress like her when I sang with the Townships. Remember?

Q2: Oh Christ yes. And don't make fun of my dick. It's not that small.

Q1: How could I make fun of something that I had so much fun with? And it is very small, relatively speaking, Coz.

Q2: Don't call me that! We're distant cousins.

Q1: We didn't use to be, sweetheart.

Q2: Cut it out!

Q1: Everyone in that area is related somehow. Remember Kinmount?

Q2: Everyone on earth is related somehow. That doesn't mean you have to broadcast it. And why the hell does she want to photograph Jolene?

Q1: She's a painter now. She's very good. And she wants to do a portrait.

Q2: You still have her?

Q1: She's in the closet.

Q2: Of course she is.

Q1: Maybe I should just give her to Hannah.

Q2: Where did you find her in the first place?

Q1: I was doing a show at a hair salon, the Bar Beside.

Q2: A show in a hair salon?

Q1: Yes. It was lovely. Two lesbians ran it. They had a bar and small stage at the front. It was huge, filled with sofas and wing chairs and all kinds of fabulous clutter—vintage wig stands everywhere, and turquoise Hamilton Beach hair dryers.

Q2: Hamilton Beach made hair dryers?

Q1: How the hell should I know. But that's how I remember those hair dryers. They were the same colour as Hamilton Beach blenders, or something inanimate and memorable from my drug addled past. I did my little AIDS monologue there, at the Bar Beside. The stylist, one of the lesbians, was gorgeous, looked like Frida Kahlo, without the uni-brow. And the bartender, Frida's business partner and lover, looked like a very handsome version of Diego Rivera. They were quite the couple.

Q2: Are they still together, running the salon?

Q1: No. That's why I got custody of Jolene. She was sitting there, amongst all that beautiful clutter, on a treacherous glass shelf. And while I was rambling through my interminable little comic AIDS monologue each night I could see Jolene sitting there, in her hot pink heels and her bustier and that tremendous trail of soft pink tulle jutting from her behind, her legs crossed, ornaments on her antlers, looking so smug and self-assured, when really, underneath the gloss, the drag, she seemed like such a melancholy creature, at odds with her own fabulous identity. And she would watch my show, every night, against her inanimate little will, loving every maudlin self-mocking hilarious minute of it, and I knew Jolene wanted me to take her home with me. So just before the end of the run of my show, I asked Frida if I could buy Jolene from her. I named her Jolene after the Dolly Parton song, such a closeted queer lyric that one. And she was so kind. She just gave her to me. I had her out for years, but people always made fun of her when they came to visit, said she looked like some outrageous Christmas decoration. So I put her in the closet. And now Hannah wants her, for a portrait. So maybe I should just let her go.

Q2: Do you remember that hair salon we saw in Miami that time? I think you took a photo.

Q1: What the fuck are you talking about now?

Q2: When we went to Miami in the nineties. We were still madly in love. Remember?

Q1: No. I have no memory of being madly in love with you whatsoever.

Q2: We were in Miami. You remember. It was wonderful. We rarely left the hotel room, right on the beach. The twenty-fourth floor. You kept singing *Don't Cry for me Argentina* from the balcony between blowjobs, among other things. One afternoon we went for a walk, and you noticed a hair salon. When you mentioned Hannah it reminded me. It was called *Hannah and Her Scissors*. And you took a photo.

Q1: Yes, I'm beginning to formulate a vague memory of that, as you speak. But I still do not recall the part about being in love. I've got it! Ev Love. My new drag name.

Q2: It's awkward, has no rhythm.

Q1: It's an anagram, Ev Love. For evolve.

Q2: It's obscure and awkward. I think Lana Anal Is better.

Q1: Sure, why not. How bout we go the whole sixty-nine yards and just have full blown sex.

Q2: I'd have to take my wig and make-up off. You never liked doing it when I was in drag.

Q1: Leave it on, sweetheart. I've changed.

Q2: You've evolved?

Q1: Yes, Love. I've evolved.

I Don't Know How to Love

Should I speak of love, let my feelings out?
I never thought I'd come to this.
What's it all about?

—Tim Rice

It's an old story and not a very interesting one. A man of a certain age suddenly comes to the realization that he has had so much casual sex with acquaintances and strangers, and so little with people he has gotten to know, that he has developed no real talent for conversation with long-term lovers. So he starts to make a conscious attempt to talk to the people he is sleeping with. The list is considerable. He is still attractive and has no difficulty finding other 'like-minded' individuals. And except for one ill-chosen remark about hair colour during sexual intercourse, in the eyes of the seventeen-odd people he is currently seeing, there is no noticeable change in his inter-personal skills. His sexual cohorts have never noticed him lacking in the art of social dialogue before. But therein lies the problem. To him, it seems like dialogue—on the page. He is reciting it like a well-trained film actor. Not too loud, not too emotive, the camera will do some of the work for you. When the time is right an out-pouring of emotion will be extracted carefully and subtly. This isn't the stage. You don't have to project, or reach the heart and soul of the shop girl in the back row of the balcony with the windows to your soul. She—the filmgoer of your dreams—will desire you wholeheartedly if you simply follow the foolproof maxim—less is more.

But he doesn't feel them deep inside—the things he says— and can't figure out why. He's had so many women before, and although in very many ways each new encounter is just one more, he has always prided himself on his special love for all of the women he has slept with. So now, at the moment in his life when he has decided to make a conscious attempt to develop new social skills around intimacy, why does it all seem so hollow and unfelt? Because he has already done it by rote so many times in a world that privileges the concept of one-and-only? And by considering the emotional trappings of the so-called 'normal' world of courtship and romance so late in life, has he inadvertently rendered himself a mere shell of a man filled with nothing but the memories of extreme sexual fulfillment with a variety of beautiful and exciting women?

He doesn't believe any of that crap. He looks around at his men friends and sees their long-term relationships and they are not all trainwrecks. But they are also not entirely fulfilling. There is nothing wrong with them. They just don't strike him as something he longs for. So he decides to carry on with the business of learning how to consciously speak tenderly and meaningfully to people he knows—the people he is already sleeping with and the people he may one day sleep with after learning, through heartfelt conversation, all kinds of wonderful things about them. This does not stop him from continuing to sleep with near-strangers. With time they may become the people he knows. He is simply making a mid-life adjustment, akin to buying a new belt when you feel your old ones are all just a little too tight. They feel fine, but they could expand a bit. He is aware of the objectifying nature of his metaphors but does not feel that they present a problem in his daily life. He knows that a woman is not a belt.

So now, when he walks into rooms with a paramour that none of his men friends have ever seen before, and he notices their smirky smiles, with a trace of envy marking their tone of voice when they greet him, he always remembers to introduce his date by clearly stating her full name and her profession. It may seem a small step to many, but in his world it is a giant foot forward, as he comfortably and confidently makes his way toward the end of a life that he has absolutely no intention of ever making any apologies for.

35

Yellow Magic, Calming Air

They waited.
The door did not open.
The rain did not stop.
The darkness made a tent
and covered them completely.
　　　　　—Timothy Findley, *Not Wanted On The Voyage*

Sitting down—silent—on the fibreglass bench, he looked pale as his towel, his reddish hair damp, lifeless. Pressing his knuckles against the hard plastic surface, he sat on his fists until his hands turned white—then he lowered his head and stared at the floor of the steam room.

He could hear someone whisper, with a slight soft giggle in their tone: "Ginger." He thought he was talking to him. But when he raised his eyes slightly, to see, he decided it was someone making fun of him—or trying to flirt. But the stranger wasn't talking directly to him. He was whispering to someone sitting beside him, both raising their eyes surreptitiously, through the mist, trying to catch his gaze, but he never looked up long enough.

Softly—"Ginger."

Flirting seemed like the wrong term for this kind of environment. Making fun of someone's hair colour seemed far too juvenile for the unbridled, pseudo-sophistication of a men's steam room where straight and queer mixed and mingled—few questions asked, even fewer answered. Quiet worship and subtle, sometimes robust play, stroking each other's beautiful necks, running palms through full warm manes of wet hair, the round erotic flow of a shaven head and the exposed crevasse of an unsheltered ear.

It must be flirting—or a bit of both. Flirting combined with slight, titillated mockery. In his experience, some people responded to redheads like that—with a mixture of dread and desire.

There were eight men, four on each bench. Four more could fit before it filled to capacity, but he didn't know that because he hadn't read the sign beside the door—and because he had never been to this particular site before. He had followed the PATH all the way from the Fairmont, connected to the train station, snaking itself underground to the Greyhound terminal. He only had to walk a few blocks outdoors to reach the desired destination.

And when he arrived, shed his clothes, and joined the ranks, it suddenly all seemed very Christian to him. Four short of an Apostolic gathering, sitting on benches across from like-minded individuals, relaxing after supping, waiting for something that might never materialize, nervous that a few resistant non-zealots may be hiding in a small crowd of chosen 'faggots.' Loving the word 'faggots' because it spoke of an appropriated muse who resisted hate and all hate stood for. Being christened by droplets from the sweating ceiling of a small chapel-like room. It was very religious. All they needed was some church music, or opera. Eh?

This was the only central location, notorious for its posh, exclusive, over-priced membership-plus section with the free coffee, cable TV, complimentary toiletries, and all the towels you could use during a single visit. Lockers for overnight storage, a private sauna, steam room, and workout facility with a variety of weight machines, treadmills, stationary bikes, and cardio-enhancing trainers.

He had always just said Y. But he liked the combination of all four letters. Together they sounded like a complete sentence—like a question beginning with the word why and ending with a particularly Canadian interjection—eh.

"Why Em see, eh?"

"Because she has eyes."

Or when he would call his best friend—drag name: Angel Lake—to join him on the elliptical trainer at his neighbourhood location closer to the west end river area. 'She' would always come in full make-up and hot-pink workout shorts, a white tank top and runners with red flashing lights in the soles, her long highlighted bronze hair teased and teasing to within an inch of its life.

"Hi. I'm at the Y."

"Why?"

"Why not? Wanna join me?"

"Why?"

"Why not?" (*irritated, royal, pause*) "Get over here, Bitch. We both need to work out and it's a lot more fun when you're here."

She would arrive twenty minutes later, walk straight to the elliptical trainer, put one earphone in, listen to music and chatter away to him about this, that, and the other thing—and inevitably, like clockwork, every time they met, at some point she would interject, into the conversation, as natural as can be, looking straight at her depressive, conservatively-dressed best friend in his tight white V-neck gym shirt and his Adidas track pants and his white Nikes—

> *Young man, there's no need to feel down.*
> *I said, young man, pick yourself off the ground.*
> *I said, young man, 'cause you're in a new town,*
> *there's no need to feel down.*

This predictable, contrived repartee always made him laugh, and think of the time, years earlier, when he took his nephews to the water park at the community centre in suburban Calgary. They were all just minding their own business, splashing around in the big pool with all the families frolicking about. He had just been on a harrowing waterslide with his youngest nephew who screamed with laughter the whole way down the slide, only a few feet ahead of him, prostrate, limbs flailing in a thin layer of water rushing through the huge plastic tunnel.

He was always afraid of tunnels as a child, but for some reason, waterslides had never bothered him. Until this one. It was unusually dark, and he was instantly terrified as he pushed off into a swirling corridor of watery doom—suppressing the urge to scream all the way down. He didn't want to embarrass himself in front of his nephew. But when they got back to the big pool, and the music competition started, he couldn't resist taking part, prompting all three of his young wards to scurry out of the water and hide in the change room. They knew their uncle was a mad bent diva but they had no idea what it would look like in a pool, with iconic musical accompaniment.

Over the loudspeaker, the manly voice of a lifeguard wearing what looked like a vintage Speedo filled with a jam-packed basket that would put the food bank to shame—

"The best dancer will win a big prize. Is everybody ready? Get set. Go!"

And the music began. At first he couldn't believe his ears. Did these people even know the origins of the song? Apparently not. Moms and dads, toddlers in their arms, pre-teens and even some tattooed older boys and their bejewelled girlfriends hanging off the side of their adolescent beaus' torsos, laughing and singing along, as they all tried to do the best YMCA dance they possibly could. Village people? This was a full-fledged community of wild water babies gone viral.

First letter—arms raised on an angle above your head, straight and tense, bent outwards. No slouching. Y? Y not?

Second letter—that weird heart-like curve of both upper limbs that didn't really look like an M, more like some misshapen pretzel M, but it was the best the human body could muster.

Third letter—the claw-like curve of both arms to make a strange, bumpy C-like configuration, with your head in the middle, ruining the perfect swerve of the arms.

Fourth letter—the triangular shape of upper limbs above

the head and joined in a peak with palms extended and fingertips taut and touching. Eh?

> *Y. M. C. A. … Just go to the Y.M.C.A.*
> *Young man, are you listening to me?*
> *Young man, young man, what do you wanna be?*

By the end of the song, he was breathless—would have been sweating had it been on dry land. He looked around, and a few people were staring. His nephews were nowhere in sight. As he waded out of the pool, he could hear the teenaged squeals of the winners who were on the pool deck beside the lifeguard getting their big prize—a pair of goggles? What a massive disappointment that must have been when a six pack of beer, a boatload of condoms, and a couple of hours in the parking lot in the back seat of an air-conditioned car with the pick of the bikinied litter would have been a far more appropriate reward for dancing mindlessly to an anthem-like tune that spoke in guarded narrative strains about the carnal camaraderie of men fraternizing at a once exclusively same-sex site for Christian associates and other like-minded biological male spirits and their crucified soulmates.

But thoughts of past outings with his nephews, two thousand miles away, were the furthest thing from his mind. He was sitting in a steam room he had never been in before, doing something he had never done before, and he was having second thoughts.

* * *

"Ginger."

It was a little louder the third time, probably because there were fewer men in the steam room. Just the three of them—'Ginger' and the two ginger-loving fellows across from him.

They separated, sliding subtly away from each other on the

bench, leaving about eighteen inches between them, just room enough for another body, with a few inches to spare. Then the one on the right rested his palm on the bench, gently patting the empty space and looking straight at Ginger. Ginger didn't look up, but his eyes were not completely averted. That haunting way the retina and pupil have of turning slightly upwards without much movement in the outer area of the eye—the lid, upper and lower, remaining almost completely still, and the encasing head also still, where eyes reside—just slight vertical movement allowing one to gain enough vision to view the light moans and small startling squeals, the *"eee! eee!"* 'cum-ings' and goings of something lurid and lovely happening only inches away.

"Ginger." Followed by another set of light taps on the bench, from the stranger's flattened palm.

Nonplussed—only slightly ruffled—and very timid, Ginger took his extra towel from his shoulders and rubbed his head. To his unpleasant surprise, there were faint yellow streaks on the white cotton cloth. It was the light red rinse he had used in the hotel room the night before. This was embarrassing. If he did what those ginger lovers wanted him to do, fill that empty space between them—and play along, thrilling them softly with his schlong—they might touch his head and discover the secret only his hairdresser knew for sure. He had the right complexion for a redhead. It didn't look fake. But he couldn't risk it. So he got up slowly and started to walk toward the steam room door.

"Ginger. C'mon. Please."

And then the stranger on the left gently tugged at the second towel that Ginger had carelessly let drag behind him as he tried to exit. Ginger stopped, then turned, then caved.

Sitting between them quickly became a scene from what one might describe as three horny entangled muses out for an afternoon of lust, goodwill, and rococo-like bodily charm—this way and that way, all akimbo, graceful and skewed in their heavenly sculpted moves.

The two cohorts kept muttering flattering endearments under their breath, and then it happened.

"What the fuck?"

The one on the left had run his fingers through Ginger's hair, trying to subtly guide his head toward his own crotch. But Ginger wasn't having any of that, and as he quickly pulled his head away he noticed a yellowish tinge on the stranger's palms.

"Are you kidding me?"

In the steam, the reddish hue spread into a thin light amber tone—yellowish. The mist gave the overall impression of something faint and magical in the air, floating just above the surface of the flesh. A calm film of ethereal powder, damp and gently winging it through a sweet translucent atmosphere, like wafts of sacred substance drifting through a church. Eh?

"He dyes his hair, and then he goes to a steam room. Is he nuts?"

"Calm down, Henry. He's very cute."

Ginger thought to himself, 'I may be the third person, but I am not *in* the third person. Talk to me, not about me. I'm here, I'm queer, sitting right between you two ginger-loving jackasses. Be nice. I'm new to this kind of thing. I usually only engage in this type of behaviour in large city parks, in foreign countries—preferably the Mediterranean—or with hookers in expensive hotels in upstate New York—Albany or Syracuse, the odd time Schenectady because I love the sound of that word.' But Ginger kept his thoughts to himself as sweat thickened on his brow.

Once Henry calmed down about the streaks of dye, and the air had grown thicker with bursts of steam that renewed themselves every quarter of an hour, the threesome began again—a kind of misty tableaux vivant of three graces, having fallen. Faith was blowing him, lapping his hard cock like some engorged crucifix, crossed by Ginger's ample balls, the rest of the priestly object comprised of a finely grown shaft of light hair from the base of his penis to just above his navel. Hope was servicing Ginger's butthole with a single index finger thrust fully, with spit, into the tightening sphincter as Charity, aka Ginger, sat contented in the middle.

Although relatively new to all of this, Ginger took to it like a duck to water, so to speak. He swiftly grabbed his own balls tightly, cupping them in his palm, increasing the pleasurable sensation of having his cock proficiently sucked, stabilizing the array of sensations and focusing on the desired orgasm, his head tilted back slightly against the steam room wall. When he came his eyes were closed and all action on both sides had ended, several seconds before the erotic explosion. He moaned, opened his eyes, and looked around. There was no one there. Faith and Hope were gone.

Standing up quickly, slightly stunned by his own behaviour, but fulfilled, then sitting back down—silent—on his solid fibreglass seat, he looked pale as his towel, his reddish hair damp, lifeless. Pressing his knuckles against the hard plastic surface, he sat on his fists until his hands turned white—then he lowered his head and stared at the floor of the steam room.

> *His palms bled yellow,*
> *nailed by his buttocks to*
> *the hard submissive surface*
> *of the damp spent bench.*

The Origin and Tonic
of the Word Flu

Once, a very long time ago, in the distant past, bordering on the present, dangerously close to the future, threatening to become a phenomenon for all time, two virile men were talking. One was tall and handsome, and the other one was short and extremely good-looking. If an historic medical diagram were to be made, similar in proportion to da Vinci's drawing of the perfect man, and if you turned the short man upside down and placed him beside the tall man, with the short man's feet positioned at the tip of the tall man's head, then the short man's head would be placed precisely at the point at which the tall man's crotch would be located. There is nothing homosexual about this observation. It is a simple fact that the two men in question discovered one night when, in their thirties, they had no luck at a popular pickup bar for heterosexuals, so they went home together and attempted to give each other a blowjob. They failed miserably and threw up after the attempt. The projectile regurgitation of previously ingested food stuffs was due more to the combination of nachos, beer, a gin and tonic, and six vodka shooters each, and less to the shock of suddenly discovering that sucking cock was not as stomach turning as they had been led to believe. During their neophytic encounter, the tall man said, at one point, "I never realized how short you are. Your feet are precisely at the top of my head." And the short man replied, "But how is that possible? You are sucking my cock, and I am sucking yours?" And that is the point when the tall man began to throw up, and the sound of his virile friend retching prompted the short man to throw up as well. So the question of the proximity of the short man's feet to the tall man's head was never proven or, for that matter, disputed or raised ever again in their lifetimes—well, almost. For the most part they simply carried on as if nothing out of the ordinary had ever occurred between them.

As they grew older, the memory of this encounter grew so dim that it became an unsung fable lying dormant in the far reaches of their gin-soaked brains. But one night, the fable was unearthed, when the tall man, feeling exhausted and achy and sniffling and sneezing the whole night long as they guzzled gin and watched all the young women pass them by at their favourite pickup bar, began to remember, in graphic detail, the night of the largely forgotten and utterly unmentionable pseudo-erotic encounter that had happened between them so many years ago. But instead of simply recounting the story to his buddy, the tall man instead began to beard his memories with a burst of testosterone-induced bravado.

"I was feelin' up this little floozy the other night, and I . . ."

And in the middle of a sentence that was intended to impress his short friend with the breadth and scope of his virility, the tall man fainted dead away, literally. He had been suffering from a severe flu that turned out to be a rare strain. It had suddenly reached his brain, and he had been hiding his suffering from every-one for weeks. He had been closeting his fever in gin after gin after gin after gin. If he had just stayed home and nursed his ailment properly, he would have died peacefully in his sleep.

But there he was, dead on the floor of his favourite pickup bar, without someone to go home with. The short man looked down and laughed, thinking his friend was dead drunk. In a sense, he was correct. But the next day, his shifting mid-fifties physiology prompted him to cry more for his tall dead friend than he had ever cried before. Surges of mid-life estrogen were having their way with him like never before.

"What on earth happened?" was the general cry from all the

tall man's friends when they shook the hand of the short man at the funeral line-up and comforted him in his profound homo-social grief.

Sputtering through endless sobs and crying jags the short man replied, "Well, I don't know for sure. I was a little tight myself that night, and all I remember is that he was talking about feeling a little flu-ey, and then he passed out. I had no idea how sick he was."

So it turns out that the word flu originated from a misunderstanding between a tall man and a short man. The tall man said floozy and the short man thought he said flu-ey. And since the tall man was dead soon after the misunderstanding occurred, then the misunderstanding could never be cleared up, and floozies, through no fault of their own, have had a bad name ever since.

Pair a Bulls

Two widowed cows were sitting in a field, lamenting the loss of their husbands.

"I told them not to move to Spain, but those morons wouldn't listen to us."

"I couldn't agree more. I have nothing against Spain, but it is not a good place for two bulls to move to in their prime. They're just asking for trouble."

And as the sun set and the remains of the day languished in the far west end of the barnyard, the lady cows made their way in an organized and humane fashion, through the maze of high technology that gently and carefully directed them to their slaughter. Temple Grandin had lovingly paved the way for these bovine beauties to meet their destiny in as circular and serenely a way as humanly possible.

As the final glimmer of a blazing crest of sunlight disappeared behind the rural tree line, one of the lady cows said to the other, with udder and complete dissatisfaction, "Even if we had wanted to, they never would have let us go to Spain with them. But I did enjoy that china shop they took us to just before they left. I'm a real sucker for those Royal Doulton figurines of the fancy ladies in flowing gowns and glamorous upsweeps tucked under their lovely hats. And the one he bought me, of that tiny kitten licking its little white paw: I may never see him again, but I will cherish it until the day I die. It's hidden under a favourite cow pie by that stand of willows we both loved to lounge under on sunny days." And the other cow smiled and shook her head in agreement, saying lovingly, "Yes, it was beautiful, all that precious china, and we broke so many lovely things."

They both fondly reflected upon the departure of their beloved bulls as they trod along, gaily, toward destiny.

Home & School

If you like piña coladas and getting caught in the rain
If you're not into yoga, if you have half a brain
If you like making love at midnight in the dunes of the cape
Then I'm the love that you've looked for, write to me and escape.
—Escape (the Piña Colada song)

"They're crab lice dear."
She was so lovely, and very sensitive to his situation. He had never seen one before. So when he noticed the itching, he shaved his pubes, picked a single tiny speck from his flesh, saw that it was moving, put it in a Dixie cup, covered it with Saran, and placed it on top of the dresser. When he left the house the next morning, for an early class, he slipped it into his backpack and headed for the bus. His mother was sleeping on the pullout couch in the family room, with the television on. She was rarely awake when he left. Tom and Jerry were having their way with a field mouse.

* * *

At the campus clinic, his innocence was disarming. She concealed her laughter with a charming smile and just told him what it was lying dormant at the bottom of the little cup.

"I do wash my mother's clothing. It could have come from there."

"No dear, I don't think so. Have you had any sexual contact lately?"

"Yes. I was in Toronto last weekend."

"That's probably where you picked it up."

As she scrawled barely-legible letters on a slip of paper, he remembered that night at the baths, his very first time. Ethel Merman was singing disco versions of all her greatest Broadway hits as he wandered aimlessly, an eager neophyte, with no idea of how he should behave. To raucous strains of *Everything's Coming Up Roses* and *There's No Business Like Show Business*, he gritted his teeth, concealed his nervousness with an aloof indifference, and headed for the darkened hallways. He even knocked on closed doors, not knowing that the opened ones signified availability and the closed ones were in full-blown usage. It had been a night to remember— the cock ring he initially thought was surgically attached to the stranger's balls until it snapped off mid-coitus revealing a three domed strap of leather that heightened the erection as it flopped and bounced between his thighs. The ribbed condom he thought was used and filthy until he unwittingly discovered it was tinted and infused with a light chocolate flavour. An adventurous night away from home and school, filled with sex education of the encountering kind.

* * *

"It's a lotion dear. The instructions are very simple. You can buy it over the counter at any pharmacy."

"Great, thanks. I'll get it this afternoon, after I finish my Virginia Woolf essay."

As he turned to go, she gently touched his sleeve. He had visited her office many times, and although she was a part-time campus GP, she was willing to listen to whatever he felt the need to say. His first therapist of sorts.

"Dear, you've done well by your mother. She's lucky you're there, for the time being, living with her." He smiled, politely thanked her, and left.

Buying the remedy for crab lice at the pharmacy where his mother worked part-time was probably not the best idea. But strangely, it never occurred to him that they would know its purpose.

* * *

For the rest of his life, he would remember the doctor's kind words, and whenever he thought of that lotion, long into middle-age, he would think of one of his favourite cocktails—a Piña Colada. The words sounded so similar, colada and Kwellada. He would drink a few, laugh an inebriated little laugh, think of that lovely doctor, raise his glass in the air, mutter "penis Kwellada" to himself, and bask in the afternoon sun, thanking goddesses and goodness for all of the precious time and all of the jaded innocence he had left to encounter in the world.

Age & Innocence

He didn't know what shade of blue those loafers had been. All he remembered was that they were like no other colour he had ever seen before. All creamy and smooth and matching his American History teacher's satiny tie. Maybe robin's egg blue, but not really. They lacked the brightness of robin's egg, had a softer quality to them, with a little gold buckle across the arch of each foot—and just a glimpse of matching socks, just a shade lighter than the loafers. Perhaps they were teal, or aqua, or turquoise. He always had such trouble sorting out the blues.

The American History teacher's hair was grey and full, like his wife's, the guidance counsellor. She told him he could never be an interior decorator because his math was so bad he wouldn't even be able to measure drapery material. There was a tone of indignation in her gruff, matronly voice, even when she said the most absurd and discouraging things. She looked beautiful and stately, a powerhouse of stern femininity, like her husband in butch lesbian drag. They had no children and had met in teachers' college. She had a full, grey head of hair too, but her fashion sense was not quite as good as his. He worked in make-up at the local theatre guild, and she always talked about the plays he worked on. They both felt Beckett was too bleak and preferred Shakespeare's comedies—never really wanting to see anyone die onstage.

It was the year Nixon was impeached and the American History teacher asked the whole class if they thought the President deserved this kind of treatment. He didn't know what to say. He couldn't

comprehend any of it. Just sat there embarrassed that he understood so little about the world, and barely passed from one grade
to the other. They put him into the trades curriculum, and one boy
awkwardly asked—with a hint of strained teenaged innocence
mixed with an outrageous air of stupidity— asked him if he had
a sister who looked as pretty as him. He said no, and then went
back to spoiling a perfectly good piece of wood on a treacherous
lathe he had no idea how to use properly. But he was always good
in English Literature, and they pushed him through high school,
only holding him back one year because he was so small and bash-
ful that no one would ever notice, and maybe he would grow into
himself, catch up to the others. But everyone knew it would never
really be possible.

He was good in English though. They just called it English
then, unapologetically, like it made perfect sense, as if the world
only had one language and all great literature was based in it. His
life then was like a bad education system. Shutting out so many
things that would become his biggest concerns as an adult. One
teacher altered his opinion of Daisy Buchanan one day in class,
when he spoke out against the teacher's belief that Daisy was just
a superficial creature. He raised his hand, and once the teacher
acknowledged him, he said softly, with a slight boyish tremor, "She
knew, she knew how awful the world was. So she wanted her
daughter to be a beautiful little fool so she would never know just
how terrible people could be, including herself."

It was the mid-seventies, and it seemed like a very small
world to him, in the midst of his blighted family life and the loss
of a tormented parent. The Second World War was barely two
decades cold and the rest of that century's war years were brewing
in places he had never heard of. He watched his father's wounds
fester in the bottom of empty bottles and unfulfilled loins. And
his mother. She was another short story—another poem—waiting
to be written, by him, over and over again.

"Would you like to come to my house on Friday evening?

We could chat. You've had a difficult time since your dad died. My wife will be out for the evening. We could just have a nice talk."

Innocence was something he wore, like the tight light blue, brushed denim bell bottomed trousers everyone stared at when he walked into the classroom. Many years later a teacher he had never studied with told him, at a local queer-friendly bar in his hometown, "You were so small, and so beautiful then. It was like you were going to fly away at any moment." The things people say so long after the fact. He was mildly disgusted by the nonchalance of so many of the latent thoughts that could never have been uttered at the right time. But there was a kind of delayed thrill, hearing how he had once been perceived and objectified.

He sat in his American History teacher's den in a chair near the fireplace, and they chatted. The moment his innocence sputtered, then burst, was when that great throbbing head of grey hair leapt then bobbed suddenly in his lap, against the zipper of his tight jeans, flared at the hem. He pulled away quickly and said "no"—nervously, with a subdued shock in his voice, and remembered his teacher's words for years after—as he had quickly come toward him and knelt down, mid-conversation.

"Well, now that I know why you're here."

But even then, and through all the years that passed, he never knew what it was that had been said to make his teacher initiate that sudden movement from small talk to a quick leap into his lap. He was eighteen, very small for his age; innocence was like clothing to him. He just put it on and took it off, according to the time of day, and barely noticed the change. But he was always aware of the colour coordinates. Blues—all kinds—were his favourite then.

"It's my wife, isn't it? If she wasn't in the picture?"
The student nodded—not knowing why he was nodding—and his teacher went back to his chair. He drove him home soon after. They barely spoke, but there was a kind of comfort between them. They did know each other in a way that no one else dared to.

No one ever asked about the meeting. It was just a kindly

teacher taking an interest in a student who had suffered sudden trauma in his young life. And what had he done wrong, really? Nothing. It just wasn't in the cards. But there was something reassuring in the innocent knowledge that the next time he went into the guidance counsellor's office, she would have a very different effect on him. It was a tiny moment of paradise when he realized she could never move him to tears in the way she had before his meeting with her husband. There would be no power lost and no power gained. They were both innocent, for a moment, then, and neither one of them would ever really know why.

Transit Story

The onanist picked up a transfer that was lying on the floor of the streetcar. Pressing it between his thumb and forefinger, he began to think of the last time he had spilled his seed. There had been an anti-climax, but the events leading up to the end were quite provocative.

After pondering the limp ending of an auto-erotic narrative for a few moments, he remembered another story, one that his mother had told him, of a young man who would not do as his father bid him, and he went blind. It frightened him as a child, and then, later, as a teenager, he worked in a movie theatre as an usher. It was 1974 and a British comedy came to town called *If You Don't Stop It You'll Go Blind*. He saw the film several times, standing at the back of the theatre. It was filled with sketch comedy scenes of old ladies espousing profane activities, gay cowboys entangled in compromising acts, and competitive sex contests filled with horny blokes and well-endowed beauty queens—among other things.

He was twenty at the time and a late bloomer. A late bloomer who had found himself in a variety of compromising positions. Once he stood at the urinal in the men's washroom of the Odeon Theatre, where he worked for a year just before his father died, and he saw a man playing with himself and looking straight down into the porcelain altar. He went back to his post at the back of the theatre and reminisced briefly about the size of the stranger's massive member.

A few years later, the film was followed by a sequel, *Can I*

Do It 'Til I Need Glasses? He never saw that one, and didn't need glasses himself until he was in his late forties. By the time he reached his mid-fifties, he was buying cheap reading glasses at the dollar store. When he was fifty-eight, he had graduated from a two hundred lens to three hundred and fifty. When he watched porn on his laptop, he left his glasses on. But when he actually took part in full-fledged autoerotic acts, his spectacles were left on the bedside table.

* * *

As the sleek twenty-first-century streetcar sailed along with seamless agility, so unlike the rattling old trolleys he first rode in the nineteen-seventies, he pressed the filthy transfer softly between his fingers and started to become self-conscious about the filth and germs that must be all over the little slip of grey paper. So he dropped it back on the floor, and as he did so, a stranger glared at him and shouted, "Don't litter." He considered a variety of responses, but luckily the streetcar was at his stop, so he just ignored the stranger's indignant outcry and made his way to the exit. The stranger kept shouting long after he had left. But that was neither here nor there.

When he entered the lobby of the hospital, he went straight to the hygiene station near the entrance and squeezed a sizeable dollop onto both palms, vigorously pressing the alcohol-based liquid into his skin. There were light abrasions at the ends of his fingertips that stung a little as the substance was absorbed. The abrasions had been the result of a failed attempt to get Crazy Glue off his skin with sandpaper. It just left little cuts between the dried, hard puddles of toxic adhesive. He hated Crazy Glue and tried not to use it often. But there were times when it seemed to be the only solution for the reinvention of a beloved broken object.

He then walked to the west end of the main floor of the hospital, took a sharp left, went up the escalator to the second floor, and walked straight down the hall to the elevators, where he stood and waited for one to take him to the ninth floor. After waiting ten minutes for the doctor to retrieve him from the depressing little windowless waiting room, he walked over to the receptionist's office and asked an employee to let the doctor know that he had arrived. And then he went back to the waiting room and saw his doctor standing there looking around. They saw each other, smiled, and then went to the office together.

When he put his pants back on, the doctor was standing by the window, gazing out at the downtown skyline.

"Hey Doc, I heard a joke the other day that reminded me of you. You wanna hear it?"

"No, I don't think so. Our session is over. I'll see you next week."

"Aw, come on. It's funny, and very short."

"Okay. Tell me, quickly."

Just as he was about to start telling the joke, the doctor's phone rang. After a few words, the doctor put the phone down and told him that his next patient had just cancelled, so he could take a little more time telling the joke. They both sat down on the couch.

"So this guy went to see his doctor, and his doctor told him that he had to stop masturbating. And the guy said, but why, Doc, why do I have to stop? And the doctor said, because it makes it difficult to examine you." He laughed, but the doctor just smiled.

They had a free hour, after the joke, so they just stayed there, in the office, with the door locked. When he put his pants back on, his patient was standing by the window gazing out at the downtown skyline, thinking to himself,

'I'm glad I dropped that filthy transfer and sanitized my hands before coming up here. My father always warned me about proper hygiene, and even though his stories frightened me as a child, they sure come in handy now that I'm all grown up.'

Ganesh One

He wasn't actually seeing the images, just thinking about the possibility.

It was his favourite room in the house because of the beautiful, dark, winding stairway and all of the family photos on the walls as he climbed the stairs to the second floor. The walls had just been painted the summer before, during his first visit to the island. It was the least he could do—and he loved painting houses—since his friend was housing and feeding him for almost a month. Otherwise, he never would have been able to afford such a long holiday.

I love this room. I love this place.

He walked around the room, touched the walls, looked at the silvery creature in the built-in wall cabinet, switched on the light over the little elephant's head, and just stared at it for a few moments. He loved Ganesh because of his beautiful majestic trunk and his many arms, and it reminded him of a young man he had met in this room a year before.

Now a year later, he was back, and the young man was gone. It was late afternoon and the very hot sun was fading. A heavy morning rain had softened the heat for a few hours, but it had been like a sauna outdoors for most of the day, and yet, the long narrow shape of the room, with its high ceilings, thick adobe walls, tiny windows, and rambling flight of stairs, somehow remained cool. The room seemed like the place itself—a serene island in the middle of a tepid sea that crept out among all of the other countries in the

world. He knew that it wasn't the centre of the universe, but sometimes it felt like it was.

Ganesh belonged to Babu, the young man, and had been a
gift from another visiting friend.

For a moment, his eyes played tricks on him, and he imagined seeing the little trunk and arms waving in the dying light as it
faded on the yellow walls. Or were the walls fading from the light?
But he caught himself, reminded himself that he wasn't actually
seeing them. He was just thinking about arms, and trunks—about
being embraced by the island, surrounded by the cool blue of the
Mediterranean, like a pale yellow room filled with diminishing sunlight, as he sipped Turkish coffee and stared at the eyes and the
welcoming arms of an ancient elephant god.

Faye

He always liked white bathing suits against tanned skin.

"Will you look at that, eh? Now there's a good-looking man."

He didn't know Faye very well, but there was something that he just loved about her. Even at thirteen years old, he could identify glamour when he saw it. The way she smoked her cigarette, gestured with her arm as though the Camel Light was a natural extension of her fingertips. He adored the way she just openly expressed her attraction to his Uncle Joe, with no shame, right in front of his aunt, who would just laugh along and nag Faye about her chain smoking.

"They're coffin nails, Faye. That's what they say. They'll kill you."

Everyone smoked then. It was the early nineteen-sixties. Buses, movie theatres, planes, everywhere you went. It was just a natural part of the social scene. His uncle was smoking that day, as he stood on the dock in his white bathing suit, his dark, slicked-back hair shiny in the afternoon sun, and his tight swim trunks hugging his backside in a way that Faye obviously could not resist commenting upon. He flicked his cigarette into the glassy surface of the lake. Faye let out a sigh and motioned to her attendant lady friends.

"Well, girls, let's take a little ride over to my place. I'll freshen your cocktails and you can all have a look at my new bedspread. It set me back two hundred and fifty bucks."

They all got into the big boat tied to the little dock not far from where his uncle was standing, and Faye revved up the inboard motor, leaving behind quite a spray of lake water as they cut a gassy swath across the clear blue surface to her summer home. Uncle Joe just stood there on the dock, looking out into nowhere. He didn't even seem to notice the boatload of grown-up girls, his wife and her twin sister among them, as they laughed, sipped daiquiris, smoked fags, and disappeared into the broken crests of waves and shafts of sunlight.

* * *

His memories always came back in a haze—no sharp details, just fragments of a time and place. They tended to collapse into each other, and as an adult struck him as being impressions of a very turbulent period filled with vivid, joyful, exciting, conflicted images that he had carried with him for close to half a century.

"That really was a gorgeous bedspread. Can you imagine spending that much money on one? That Faye, she's a real character. I think her hubby must have quite the time keeping her under control." His aunt didn't seem to mind Faye's little crush on his Uncle Joe. Faye was what one might call a real old fashioned broad. She spoke her mind and said what she meant, with a welcoming magnanimous air about everything she did. And she made no bones about her prime position as the wife of a wealthy Toronto businessman.

"Eddie's a sweetheart. I love him to death, but that doesn't mean I can't appreciate a real stud like that man of yours."

* * *

And these random memories came; never a single one, but rather a mesh of fragments from a string of consecutive summers when his aunt and uncle would cross the border at the edge of Lake Erie, drive for a few hours and stay at the family cottage for a week or two. They would blur into cohesive bits of nostalgic chaos that he could play out in his mind like a stack of CDs, a medley of haunting melodies that frequently revisited him in such complicated ways. And ultimately, at the end of every memory of that time at the lake, he always ended up in the same place.

"You're so beautiful, Davey. You look so pretty."
It was played out in a field, a rocky clearing with patches of thick, wild grass, and there were white daisies and Brown-eyed Susans, and depending upon the season, the odd white or mauve trillium here and there. And he would be lying among them, beside his uncle, and the words that very troubled man said to him had somehow become the strongest and most memorable affirmation of his own femininity.

Hortense

He knew it would never happen, but they couldn't stop him from dreaming about it. So he dutifully set out the saucer with the piece of fruitcake on it, beside the glass of Coca-Cola, on the kitchen table, and then he kissed his mom and dad goodnight and went to bed.

"Get me a glass of water."

The whining sound of his older brother's voice wakened him from a deep sleep where he had been imagining baby dolls and beautiful carriages with himself at the helm, walking along the street, happy and proud to be the new owner of a pram and a lifelike china infant. Changing rapidly from thoughts of his gender-defiant desire for a doll of his own, he switched his attention back to his brother's demands. He got up from his bed, only a few feet across from his brother's identical bed, and walked across the hall to the bathroom. He took a Dixie cup from the dispenser beside the medicine cabinet, filled it with cold water, and returned to the bedroom.

"That's not enough. I want some more. Bring two this time, and think of something to sing to me when you get back."

He would sing *Old Doctor Sun* or *Sweet Hortense*. He liked singing them both, and if the first one didn't work, then maybe the second one would put his brother back to sleep. Long enough for him to have his own dreams about all of the things he desired.

> *Old Doctor Sun please shine your lovely light*
> *On the sick children, pale children, those who are in pain.*
> *Old Doctor Sun please shine your light again.*

"More. I want more. I can't get to sleep."

Oh, oh, oh my sweet Hortense.
She ain't good lookin' but she's got good sense.
I gave Hortense a diamond ring.
Boy, it was the most beautiful thing.
She got married, now I'm alone.
She gave me back the ring but she kept the stone.
Hortense has dandy teeth in her mouth,
one pointing north and the other pointing south.
Oh, my sweet Hortense.
She ain't good lookin' but she's got good sense.
Rain makes flowers pretty I hear.
I hope it rains on her for a year.
Every time I kiss Hortense
I always buy a nickel's worth of peppermints.

He could hear his brother chuckle a little as he fell asleep with the empty Dixie cups lying crumpled beside his head. But he couldn't get to sleep himself. Singing to his older sibling always got the adrenaline flowing and it became a little bedside performance that took a while to come down from when it was over. So he just lay there thinking about all of the excitement awaiting them both when they rose from bed and went downstairs.

Seven o'clock on Christmas morning came quick enough, and there it was, to his complete surprise, sitting on the kitchen counter. When he stood on his tiptoes and peeked inside he could see the baby's pale face and rosy cheeks with a little wool blanket pulled up around its neck. He couldn't believe it. They had actually bought him a doll carriage and china doll. He hadn't believed in Santa for a few years, but they still did the ritual of leaving food out for him when he delivered all of the gifts from the North Pole. The fruitcake was half eaten, and the glass of Coke was empty. But then he noticed crumbled bits of dark bread and green and red maraschino cherries on the floor beside the counter where the carriage was perched, and realized his dad had dropped the piece of cake and hadn't noticed. But it didn't matter. He had what he wanted, and the next step was to get all dressed up in his winter coat and take that doll for a nice walk around the neighbourhood in her brand new buggy. But just as he was heading for the closet in the front hall, he heard his brother whining again.

"Get me a glass of water"—and he suddenly realized he had in fact been able to fall asleep again after his medley of *Sweet Hortense* and *Old Doctor Sun.* He got up out of bed, noticing 7:00 a.m. on the clock between the beds, and tried to relish the memory of his little doll and carriage dream, and headed for the Dixie cup dispenser.

He always wished that Old Doctor Sun would pay more attention to him, and he felt so sorry for Hortense, the way his brother laughed at her when he sang the song. There was something about her that—as a child—he couldn't quite put his finger on. But he knew she was like him. She was never going to get what she really wanted, but she would spend all of her life trying to find ways to feel surprised and delighted by all of the things she did get.

She was no great beauty, according to his brother, whenever he heard the lyrics and laughingly remarked that "she musta bin pretty ugly if he took that diamond ring away from her, and she pulled the rock out with her teeth. She was a fuckin' tomboy, that Hortense."

And he was what they called a Susie Girl. And he loved Hortense. They were a pair. His brother once called her a cow right after hearing the song, and then he fell asleep. But he knew better. She was a real beauty, a bovine beauty perhaps, but a beauty nonetheless.

Go Lightly

You can love somebody without it being like that.
You keep them a stranger, a stranger who's a friend.
　　　　　　—Truman Capote, *Breakfast at Tiffany's*

　　Sometimes you just have to be in love.
He kept saying it over and over again, in the mirror, stressing different words each time he said it. First he just said it calmly and fluidly without any stresses, almost as if there were no spaces between the words:
　　sometimesyoujusthavetobeinlove
The second time he stressed the word *be*:
　　*sometimes you just have to **be** in love*
The third time he stressed the word *in*:
　　*sometimes you just have to be **in** love*
And then he just kept repeating it, about seven times, not fully conscious of stressing any letters but all the time knowing he was trying to find a way to fully understand the words he was repeating:
　　***sometimes** you just have to be in love*
　　*sometimes **you** just have to be in love*
　　*sometimes you **just** have to be in love*
　　*sometimes you just **have** to be in love*
　　*sometimes you just have **to** be in love*
　　*sometimes you just have to **be** in love*
　　*sometimes you just have to be **in** love*
　　*sometimes you just have to be in **love***

Ultimately it didn't make any sense to him, but it satisfied a sense of longing that he felt when he thought about him, how they met, how they started using the L-word so quickly, neither one of them really knowing what it meant. So when he decided to fly back to Toronto only a few weeks after that first meeting, for Valentine's Day, he was hard put to know precisely how to respond, what to do. But it wasn't like he had never seen it done before. It was everywhere, on television, in the movies, in the card shop in the lobby of the hospital. Love was for sale, especially in the weeks that came before the big day for lovers.

Whenever that day did come, he always thought of an old Valentine, circa nineteen-twenties, that he had found in an antique shop years ago. It was a drawing of a child-like couple, sitting on a swing, and the male of the species seemed to be saying something to the female of the species. And what he was saying, printed below the swinging couple, went like this:

> *I'm rough and honest, yet brave and gay*
>
> *& I need a wife in the very worst way.*
>
> *I'll love you truly and house you fine,*
>
> *If you will be my Valentine.*

Intellectually, he understood how the word *gay* had come to mean something so radically different over a relatively short period of time, but emotionally it all seemed out of whack. It was such a lovely little word that really didn't need to carry the burden of so much political intrigue all by itself. He chose not to define himself in that way. He just thought of himself as, well, he wasn't sure. But *gay*, all alone—such a sweet, innocent little word—just didn't seem to fit the bill. But one thing he did know for sure. There was a whole world out there that claimed to know precisely what all those sweet, innocent little words, like *love* and *gay*, really meant. So, instead of confusing people with his convoluted thoughts on the transitory nature of language, he just said that he was gay, and that he was in love. Because after so many years of not really knowing what it meant, he felt it was high time to look himself straight in the eye and say, "Sometimes you just have to be in love"—stressing the words *be* and *in*—underlining them in his heart—because they seemed to him to be the most important parts of the sentence and the idea. *Being* and the act of existing *inside* something. That seemed tangible somehow, so he chose to take part in it, at least until Valentine's Day, and possibly longer.

*   *   *

His low-level, largely undiagnosed OCD—he liked to refer to it as Orange County Disorder—was on the upswing just before they met, but he knew he could curb it once he arrived from Washington. But first he had to get him a gift, and that was the hard part. He knew he could perform the role of loving someone in a romantic way. He could do that. He had done it onstage a few times, in Molière and Brad Fraser plays, and had seen other people do it on numerous occasions. But what should he buy him as a Valentine's gift? He loved buying gifts, and as he walked through the mall it just popped into his head. Of course. Do the obvious thing: buy him a little heart and put it in a card. That would be sweet, and simple. And he had already bought him the blank card at the hospital gift shop with a photo of Audrey Hepburn in *Breakfast at Tiffany's* on it—the day after they had chatted on the phone and he told him he had never seen the film before. It all seemed to be coming together perfectly. But his heart skipped a beat for a fleeting moment, and he thought to himself, sardonically, 'How could any self-respecting gay man have never seen that film?' But he didn't mean it. It was just one of those *he-bitchy-gay* things he thought sometimes.

Just as he walked in the door to the row of indoor shops that crossed from Yonge Street to Bay, on his way to University Avenue where the hospital was, he remembered a little kiosk with all kinds of ornate costume jewelry. It would probably be gaudy and expensive, but why not give it a try? So he headed straight for it, and within seconds of smiling at the woman behind the counter and telling her what he was looking for, she found the sweetest little rhinestone brooch, only twenty dollars, shaped like a heart. He looked at it and grinned. It was perfect. He would like it. He could imagine him wearing it on the lapel of the royal-blue trench coat he was wearing when they first met. But then, as he looked more carefully at the arrangement of tiny stones, he suddenly noticed the small crescent moon shape in the top right corner of the heart. Just that morning he had received a text message from him:

I want to dance to Moon River *with you.*

And when he did arrive, that's just what they did on that famous night of the year set aside for lovers. And it was a wonderful three days of simple romance and uncomplicated love making. During his first visit, when intimacy seemed to be creeping up over the horizon, he sat him down in the hotel lobby and said, "Let's talk for a minute. You know I'm HIV positive right?" He nodded yes, and smiled. Without missing a beat he said, "Good, well, that's done—let's go to the poetry reading now."

When he left Toronto the first time, they had begun to send daily text messages to each other. He had saved them all, two or three a day, every day since they met, up until Valentine's Day and beyond. Everything was perfect. It had all come together, the card and the brooch, and the flower he bought at the last minute as he waited for him to come through the arrival doors.

Yes, there he stood, at Terminal 3, with a rose in his hand, thinking to himself,

'I can do this. I've never really done it before, but I can do it. I can be in love with someone, someone that is okay to be in love with. Someone who's not straight, someone who's not my uncle, someone who loves me back in an appropriate way. I'm 56 years old, and I've never done this before, not like this. So it's long overdue, it's high time. And then, once it's done, I will have experienced it, and it will have been fulfilling, and I will never have to do it again.'

And then he chuckled to himself. He wasn't really feeling as cold and calculating as his thoughts sounded. But a part of him already knew, before the three days surrounding and embracing Valentine's Day even began, that if this was the only chance he would get, then he was going to make the most of it, even though he didn't know what any of it meant, where any of it would lead.

And then there he was, ninety minutes after landing, through customs in an hour and a half. He kissed him on the lips, handed him the rose, and they headed for the parking garage, and all the time he was thinking to himself, fluidly, without stressing any of the words, like a sentence without any spaces—one long word—

sometimesyoujusthavetobeinlove

...andhewas...

Goodbye (Poetic Phallusy)

*Vulgarity is not a sin against God, but against polite society.
Between you and me, I don't give a shit about polite society.*
                                        —*Carnivale*, HBO series

"Are you jealous?"

"No."

"Why not?"

"I've never been a big fan of jealousy."

"Wow. How do you do it?"

"Well, I feel jealousy, but I'm very out of touch with my feelings, so it doesn't make much of an impact."

Toby was wearing the little heart-shaped brooch, with the crescent moon in the corner, in his profile photo. After not being able to find the photo online, Kevin telephoned Toby and asked him to send the link. They chatted for about forty-five minutes, had some lovely little romantic moments about missing each other and how they would be together again in a few weeks, and then they hung up, awkwardly but lovingly.

Sipping a glass of cheap Merlot on his tenth floor balcony in chilly spring weather, with an old kitsch rug wrapped around him—one of those ones with a stylized mountain scene and a deer or a wolf standing heroically in the wilderness—Kevin thought of two quotations from Marshall McLuhan.

We become what we behold....
When we are on the telephone, we have no body.

Kevin wasn't used to saying goodbye to someone in this way, on the telephone, someone he loved. He felt awkward and at a loss as to what words he should choose. It didn't come naturally to him, this love thing. His mind was too analytical, and it just seemed more natural to him to immediately question something rather than to simply experience and enjoy it.

He sipped the Merlot and pulled his smart phone out of the little leather Roots holder on his belt, and looked up the lyrics to *This Thing Called Love.*

> *I was a hum-drum person,*
> *leading a life apart,*
> *when love flew in through my window wide,*
> *and quickened my hum-drum heart.*
>
> *Love flew in through my window.*
> *I was so happy then,*
> *but after love had stayed a little while,*
> *love flew out again.*
>
> *What is this thing called love,*
> *this funny thing called love?*
> *Just who can solve its mystery?*
> *Why should it make a fool of me?*

He thought to himself, 'What a stupid lyric, totally dependent upon the whole, monogamous one-and-only mythology. But it has a lovely melody.'

Then he went to Facebook to search for the photo and there it was, Toby in profile, looking very handsome with his

Valentine's Day gift stuck elegantly to the lapel of his black velvet dinner jacket. But it wasn't the brooch that Kevin was looking for. It was the ejaculating dildo that shot Jack Daniel's into willing audience members' mouths that he wanted to see. Toby just happened to be wearing the brooch Kevin had given him when the photo was taken.

And there they were, Kelley and Toby, in high spirits, as a stream of booze shot from the end of the prop, grazing her ample bosom, and then into her mouth. Poetry festivals had become so diverse. Kevin remembered literary events in the past where one more dry reading of nature-ridden prose poetry would be his undoing. Sitting there, patiently listening to *Ode to a Cricket* or the majestic awe-inspiring sweep of a certain godforsaken Rocky Mountain range could be disarming, in a mind-numbing way, to say the least. *The Romance of Mount Rundle* escaped him, and he often thought a more fitting ode would be called *Colonizers' Crass Corollary on Sacred Ground*, or *Ode to a Cultural Crevasse*.

Sure, there was plenty of beautiful imagery and the odd, in-spiring reader, but more often than not the poetry Kevin had heard recited early in his career had been a little stifling, and to put it mildly, a deadly art form to be surrounded by for two solid hours (or more) at the many readings he had attended when he was first testing his wings as a spoken word artist. He never really felt that he fit in. He was always writing about cock in the context of a largely autobiographical environment where *queer* and *nature* just didn't seem to have a place to comfortably co-exist.

So when he heard that his friends had been on stage together reciting dirty poetry and spraying liquor out of phallic decanters, he was thrilled. It struck him as having an almost Dada quality about it. He imagined audience members pulling random words out of hats and creating long narrative-resistant poems while a provocative host or hostess wielded an alcoholic squirt prop, rewarding every willing member with a blast of intoxicating spirits.

Now that was more like it. He felt a profound nostalgia for a past that didn't really exist, at least not in his memory. Cole Porter, Marshall McLuhan, and Noel Coward would co-host his ideal poetry festival. And Toby would be there jacking off Jack Daniel's on whomever he chose.

When he saw Kelley later that same day, after talking to Toby on the telephone, she mentioned that Toby wondered whether Kevin would be jealous about the dildo, and seemed a little nervous after the poetry festival about his onstage antics.

"No. Of course not. I'm not jealous. You can't cheat on a cheater, sweetheart. And after the life I've lived, it doesn't seem appropriate for me to start telling people who to flirt with and who not to flirt with. I flirt with furniture for Christ's sake. But that's a whole other story more suitable to an erotic special issue of *Better Homes and Gardens*."

Kevin had been collaborating with Kelley on a chapbook of erotic poems that began with some references to furniture sex. When they had their first writing session, they considered whether Toby might like to be part of it. They wanted to call it *Glory Hole Hearts*, based on something Kevin had said to Toby in a cab when they first met, about what it meant when two very promiscuous people fell in love with each other.

"Let's put the promise back into promiscuity" is a motto Kevin had always cherished.

Two of the poems Kelley and Kevin collaborated on went like this:

Whore d'oeuvres

1/ Objects of Desire

I fisted my apartment door

I felt like such an object whore

I sucked the clit of my new divan

I felt like such a handy man

Blighted by my home décor
I decay on parquet floors
I crave the sight of window shades
I insert my cock into the blades

then move those slim slats up and down
until my knob purrs like a hound
I am a dog for cushy chairs
I love it when they cum in pairs

Inanimate sex is my salvation
it leads to my divine damnation
so come on over and watch TV
as I suck the cock of CBC

2/ Sofa Love
with cheese whiz and a baggie
I craft a little pouch
then tuck it between the cushions
and fuck my brand new couch

They had also collaborated on a long haiku that begged the question about love, fidelity, and one's innate ability to stay focused on a single lover's presence in a fragmented world filled with beautiful strangers.

haiku whore

It wasn't your ass
It was his ass, but I was
Thinking of your ass

It wasn't your cock
It was his cock, but I was
Thinking of your cock

They were not your balls
They were his balls, but I was
Thinking of your balls

They were not your lips
They were his lips, but I was
Thinking of your lips

It wasn't my plan
It was his plan—to leave you
But I tried to stay

But his ass, his cock
His balls and lips—reminded
Me so much of you

So it was kind of
Like leaving you for you, but
You weren't considered

So I guess I'm bad
But it's funny, I feel great
With someone like you

"Do you think Toby will be jealous that we're writing this together, when you mentioned the idea about *Glory Hole Hearts* to him first?"

"Well, we'll just include him. It will be a poetry writing threesome. A dirty little workshop."

"He lives so far away. Do you miss him?"

"Of course I do. But we've both lived lives when missing someone just doesn't mean the same thing that it means to a lot of people. I always loved what Doris Day said, 'I miss men, but my aim was never very good.' There's something very profound in that, something that Doris may not have even been thinking. My aim was never very good because I was never really aiming at one thing. But it was always true. I was aiming at everything, all the time. That's why I love your sister Maev so much. She gets it."

Kelley loved her sister, but they fought too much to ever be as close as Kevin had become—to both of them. She just laughed and responded to him with the excitement of remembering a treasured moment onstage. "Yeah, it's like the dildo he sprayed me with at the festival. He was spraying everyone, but somehow I still felt kind of special, getting sprayed by him."

Kevin kissed Kelley goodnight and she left after a few hours of watching the box set of *Carnivale* and writing vulgar rhymes in between episodes. The characters in *Carnivale* were such fabulous archetypes for a kind of non-traditional way of living and loving. And the nineteen-thirties dustbowl was the perfect setting for such smouldering intrigue and supernatural goings on. Kevin wanted to be the bearded lady. She was so beautiful and voluptuous, and wore a simple house dress like a gorgeous faded dusty gown—and her little pointed beard had such glamour about it, at the bottom tip of her face, framing her very nostalgic femininity with such a delicious and contrasting grace.

He went back upstairs to turn off the DVD player, sipped some wine, and began to peel away at the flaking veneer on an antique piano stool he had sprayed gold and converted into a little end table. As he picked away at the aging layer of paint and wood, his smart phone started to play *Moon River*—he picked it up, and there he was, Toby, his name emblazoned across the little screen. He stared at the letters, smiled, then hesitated for just a few seconds before answering. As much as he wanted to chat, and say sweet nothings into his current paramour's ear, he couldn't help but jump straight into the questioning process, rather than just enjoying the moment. Another line from a song sprang to mind,

Every time we say goodbye I die a little.

That Cole Porter. He was relentless.

So he just picked up the phone and dove right in, because, despite his analytic impulse, he knew in his heart that every time he said hello, he began with a silent goodbye.

Roberta

After leaving Calgary six years ago, I never saw her again. She passed away in her home country, surrounded by family, and she had the most beautiful hair I had ever cut and coloured, and I had never cut and coloured hair before I met her, or after. She just assumed I could do it. The fairy flies into the room, and within minutes of meeting him she looks across the kitchen table, lifts the box of Clairol with one hand and the scissors with another, and says—"Can you do this for me?" Delighted by her instant initiative to find a task to share with me—her son-in-law's brother—I suppressed my indignant reaction around the stereotypical assumptions people frequently make about effeminate gay men, and I responded enthusiastically, "Sure, I'd love to."

While I massaged her head with black dye and combed it out in preparation for a sizeable trim, she would roll cigars from curved sheets of tobacco sent to her by relatives all the way from the Philippines. When other family members spoke of her past, in stage whispers, it was a slightly gleeful kind of exoticizing shaming that they seemed to take semi-delight in.

"She was born in a prison in China. Her mother was Chinese and her father was Filipino. They were both imprisoned for opium-dealing."

These little tidbits made me like her more. No one, not even Roberta herself, seemed sure of her age, but it probably all began somewhere not far from the nineteen-twenties.

"She has six kids, all girls and one boy. Two of the girls

snagged white North American husbands online. The boy's always sick or in trouble and getting money from his sisters. One of them married a rich guy in Switzerland. All of Roberta's kids are from the same guy—a married man she had an affair with for twenty years, and she was his wife's best friend!"

We first met in Calgary in the late nineties not long after she had come to Canada to care for my brother's youngest son. Her daughter, my brother's second wife, was a trained nurse who could only get support-staff work in a nursing home and had to go back to work right after giving birth. Roberta was, in a very real sense, unpaid labour. In a small suburban bungalow for four— there were six of them at first, and then seven—she slept in the same bed with her youngest grandson for the first five years of his life. She acted as his mother and grandmother, and she was often made to feel unwelcome in my brother's home. From time to time, Roberta would leave for extended periods and stay with other friends who had left the Philippines for similar reasons to do with family and childcare. I always felt that she tied for first place with my mother for beauty and grace of the hard-won kind.

So I did her hair. If I sit and close my eyes, and conjure memories from that time, the most calming ones are those monthly, ritualistic moments with her in the bathroom, my hands feeling the warm water through the plastic gloves, rereading the directions from the Clairol box to make sure I wasn't screwing up, her face hard pressed against a towel as I gently wove my palms through the thickness and the blue black darkness of those shiny, lush follicles, and then the move into the kitchen for the final cut. She was a patient and appreciative subject, and would make rice and delicious fried pork for me whenever I—the misidentified neophyte hairdresser—arrived. I would make a Greek salad, and she would pick lightly at it, pushing the black olives to the side and later giving them to her middle grandson who had an overdeveloped taste for popping many of them into his mouth at the same time and almost choking on the pits.

We wouldn't talk a lot. There was a language difference that made it difficult, but we seemed to communicate very well. And when my own mother died in Calgary, not long after moving there with me, Roberta urged all of us, on the day of the funeral, to refrain from washing our hair or raking the leaves in the front yard for fear of blowing our souls away with the dead. It was part of a ritual she never fully explained, and although I respected it, I could not take part in that one. I'm way too much of a fairy to deliver a eulogy on a bad hair day.

But I could be her hairdresser. And when I overheard remarks Roberta made to her daughter about how I was just like a woman, the way I pitched in and helped with all of the wife's tasks, I let my gender politics slip away long enough to indulge her need to define me. I just decided that this was a very positive thing, these Clairol moments, so to speak, and that I would make the most of them. The sudden loss of my own mother made me acutely aware of how time never stands still long enough for all good things to come full circle between loved ones before we have to say goodbye.

Long before I met Roberta, I had already made a very conscious decision not to become a hairdresser, despite the encouragement of the people in my life who felt an appropriate 'trade' would be my lot in life. And over the years, I have felt grateful for my choice. I would have been closer to Sweeney Todd than Miss Clairol. But with Roberta, I willingly and lovingly made an exception that enriched my life with an unexpected and satisfying routine. Instead of being the demon barber of Fleet Street, I was a steel magnolia for a short period, and the blossoms of that memory, that rich and marvellous routine, have never died.

Trickster White (a monologue)

Yeah, right, ex-buddy of mine, I'm gonna get myself a wife and name her Matilda and we'll learn how to waltz. For awhile, I was thinking of getting a wife from Boston and calling her Fern, but then I got more interested in Australia and dancing and forgot all about hanging plants and tea parties. My cousin got two wives from the Philippines and they kept the names they came with, but had to change everything else about themselves.

I had this friend once who joined the Air Force and he used to say, when I was sticking my finger up his ass, "This is outside my comfort zone." Which always confused me because the sounds he was making during those encounters sure sounded like comfort to me—comfort coming from the inside. He married a girl whose name was Carrie and his mother's name was Mary and he made her change it from Carrie to Emma—her middle name—because he didn't want a wife named Carrie whose mother-in-law's name was Mary. He thought the rhyme would be awkward when he introduced them both to strangers or Air Force colleagues. He did suggest at Thanksgiving to his mother and family, before he married Carrie, that everyone start to call Mary "Marie"—but they just rolled their eyes and ignored him.

He also used to like to say "emotional transaction" like it was a banking machine instead of a simple "I love you." Like the time we went for a very long walk in the woods, and I hate long walks outdoors, I prefer walking indoors. It was near the petroglyphs, before they put those goddamned fences around them and built a stupid observation deck that looks like a suburban UFO. During the walk, he kept talking about the girl he asked to come with us, but she backed out and I finger-banged him on the carved rocks after our walk, and when I dropped him off at his place later I cried and told him I was afraid of losing him. He said that wouldn't happen, but of course it did. Now over ten years later, I realize I wasn't afraid of losing him, I was afraid of losing my mind to him, and that losing him helped me to stay sane. I still have a tenuous hold on my own sanity, but that's a hell of a lot better than no hold at all.

As we pulled up our pants and left the petroglyphs, we stopped to sign the guest book. He signed his real name, but I signed it Elizabeth Taylor. Then I added the names of Minnie and Mickey Mouse when he wasn't looking. I made all three signatures look like different handwriting so no one would know it was the same wise-guy joker doing goofy things to the guest book. But honestly, who the hell needs a guest book at an ancient sacred site. Just shut the fuck up and absorb the gorgeous remnants of the spirit world, for the love of Christ.

He looked like a cross between Linda Evangelista and Christy Turlington when he was skinny and had long hair, but had started to look more like Fred Flintstone by the time he joined the Air Force and married Carrie. Which made sense because he was a bit of prehistoric space cadet from the get-go. But I loved him, and he loved me.

But he wasn't like me. He was just experimenting, and the experiment, even though it was a hell of a lot of fun, ultimately failed. Like in chemistry class in high school, when I would look at those little flasks and those round glass things with the flat bottoms, and the skinny cylindrical tops called beakers and the Bunsen burners— and it all looked so slick and fun to play with. But I never got the hang of it, and the chemistry teacher would never let me do the experiments on my own because she knew, just from looking at me and the way I stared at all the boys in my class—and she was right on the mark—she knew that I would probably make something blow up in my face. Like I always ended up doing when I got older and kept falling in love with straight guys. They just looked so slick and fun, like all that chemistry equipment, and it was worth the effort, but it did always blow the fuck up in my face, and I have the melancholy facial scars to show for it. From loving all the wrong guys. But, as Debbie Boone sang in that godawful song that I loved, "How can it be wrong when it feels so right?"

That's what my shrink calls them, the looks I get on my face all the time, my constant sullen frowns. He sometimes calls them scars of melancholy. He's a very poetic guy—and then he laughs and we make out in his office and then he gets all nervous and tries to stop me from blowing him but always gives in. I mean, honestly, if he really thought he was not going to give in then why does he bring baby wipes and a change of underwear every time I have an appointment with him?

The last thing I remember the space cadet saying to me, when we were in a tent in the same sleeping bag, naked on the side of a hill during a summer solstice festival, was "I'm a trickster. I change." And then he fell asleep, and I spent the whole night just staring at his beautiful face and the hollow majestic curve from his jutting hipbones where they met the lower part of his torso, and his long thin legs and his tiny perfect penis, and beautiful brown hair that made him look like a white Jesus. I prefer Gauguin's Yellow Christ, but I guess a skinny-assed beautiful boyish Christ is better than nothing. And as I lay there, looking at him for the last time, for several hours, I thought to myself—no, buddy, you don't change, you experiment, and when the experiment fails, you go back to the comfort zone you came from. You are not magical like a trickster, and you are not mysterious like a rock-carving. You are white and you are transparent and you are predictable and easily placed within the colonizing pecking order, and when you soar through the air in the name of God and Country in your Air Force jets, just remember me down here on the fucking godforsaken earth, remembering you and the way you make people change their names and fall in love with the unbearable non-regrettable lightness of being in your arms when you looked like a super model and not an animated Stone Age man—and those delicious boney hips thrusting their crackling angelic presence into my palm as my slim digits satisfied your emotional and physical anal desires once upon a time, a long time ago, among ancient carvings and the pure free air of long tedious walks in the stinking woods.

As for me, I'm a happy camper with a strong grip on the greasy palms of my own primal sanity, and I prefer walking in giant malls and flying on roller coasters and soaring through indoor water parks and marrying beautiful creatures named Fern or Matilda and savouring the sweet flagrant honesty of disillusion.

Betty

"Hello."

"Hi, Sweetheart. Are you coming over?"

"We talked earlier. I'll be over tomorrow afternoon, to take you to the play. I have to go to a friend's tonight. How are you feeling?"

"My finger's still sore."

"Your finger?"

"I have a cut."

"You mentioned that last week. I thought it was getting better."

"No, it's still kind of sore."

She never complained about this sort of thing.

"Well, I can stop by on my way to my friend's place if you like."

"I don't want you to go out of your way, Sweetie. But if you could, that would be nice. It would be nice to see you. You haven't been over to see me in a while."

"I've been away, and I saw you last week. Remember? We went to the mall."

"Oh, that's right. I forgot. We had pizza didn't we? That was so nice."

There was something in her voice that alarmed him. She knew how to unconsciously manipulate with a few well-chosen words and a tone of voice that suited her semi-permanent depressive demeanour. But this was different. There was anxiety in her tone that didn't sound emotional. It sounded like physical pain.

As he walked into the lobby of the retirement home, he noticed the nursing staff, but didn't stop to say his customary hello.

He just went straight to the upper lounge, where she spent most of her afternoons and evenings watching television and chatting with friends she barely knew. After giving her a peck on the cheek, he said, somewhat abruptly, "Let me see your finger."

She was holding her left hand in a tight fist and didn't seem to want to open it for him.

"Let me have a look."

He gently took her hand in his and helped her, with just a little force, to uncurl her fingertips. It seemed to be causing her pain. But he knew from experience that he would have to be a little aggressive if any real good was going to come of this visit. It wasn't easy, making a seventy-year-old woman do what he wanted her to do. But he felt it had to be done.

"Now let me have a look…Oh my God."

He felt like crying, but the tears just weren't there as he swiftly moved into over-functional mode. The ring he had given her more than twenty years before—she never took it off—had grown too tight and severed the skin. She was not one to complain about this sort of thing, and had let the blood dry to such an extent that it had formed a scab right over the thin gold band at the back of her finger.

He stood up and gently took her arm. "We're going to the hospital. Okay?"

"Oh no, I don't think so. It will be alright."

"Come on, Honey. Let's get ready."

While she put on a sweater and changed from slippers to shoes, he called the friend he was supposed to visit that evening.

"It's totally gross and probably infected. I don't think I'll make it to your place tonight. I'm taking her to Emergency at St. Michael's. That could take hours."

"Oh dear. Poor Betty. I'll meet you there."

"Okay. If you like."

* * *

The young doctor on duty was very tall and alarmingly beautiful. When his friend arrived in the waiting room, he was just in time to go into the examination room with them. While she sat in a chair and winced, silently, the doctor tried to gently tear the scab away from the ring as slowly as possible. They both tried not to stare at his beautiful face, but it was impossible for them, and a welcome distraction to what was actually happening.

He held her free hand as the medically-trained beauty finished up by applying rubbing alcohol and healing cream to the open wound. He had already removed the ring by cutting it with what looked like very tiny gardening shears. And then he applied a bandage and told them to re-dress it every day, and if it became inflamed, they should come back, and that she might have to have a shot for possible infection.

As they left the examination room, the doctor handed her some ointment, smiled beautifully, looked at her and said—"That ring really became a part of you. Didn't it, Betty?"

"It sure did. Will I be able to get it fixed so I can wear it again?"

He looked away from the doctor long enough to comfort her and say—"Don't worry, Honey. I'll take it to a jeweller's next week."

He never did. For years afterwards, the ring just lay in her purse in the tiny plastic Ziploc bag the doctor had put it in. The memory of his alarming height and beauty, his lovely hands and the way he smiled at her—his tenderness coupled with her very subtle way of calling for help when she had telephoned mid-afternoon—the whole incident, from start to finish, haunted him. But it never occurred to anyone, not him, his friend, the young doctor, or anyone at the retirement home, to find out how this could have gone unnoticed for so long. But he knew her, and the sight of such sweet, stalwart fragility—her utter helplessness as she just sat there with her hand in a tight fist when he first arrived at the Queen's retirement home—it all made a kind of sad, alarming sense.

And the unbearable image of that crust of blood forming a bridge over the backside of the tiny gold band he had given her, with four birthstones in front—mother, father, and two sons—pearl, ruby, aquamarine, and peridot. That wound—it seemed so small and so monumental at the same time. The sheer physical beauty of the young doctor distracted him and his friend long enough for them to simultaneously observe—and ignore—a licensed angel's handiwork as they watched and winced while the tall, sweet medical practitioner softly cut away at the upper edge of Betty's tortured palm.

Food for Thought (a monologue)

I was walking down Church Street the other day with my friend Dirk, and we were discussing his past as a part-time hooker and a full-time drug addict. He had been a part-time hooker to support his full-time drug addiction. He's recovering now, but sometimes it's fun to talk about the bad times because in retrospect they were a lot of fun. And even not in retrospect, they had their fun moments. It's just too bad that kind of thing always turns to shit.

I had just served Dirk a lovely meal of cod and baked potatoes, and thick tomato slices layered with bocconcini and pesto sauce, and fresh basil leaves and balsamic and olive oil, and some sour cream mixed with yogurt and sprinkled with chives atop a lovely baked russet potato. Afterwards, we went to the international coffee shop and had butter tarts and cappuccinos, and I instantly hated the teenaged server who talked to me like I was an introverted soft-spoken old fag, which of course I am—all of that—sometimes. The fact is that I wasn't, in fact, even talking to him at the time. He said, "I can't hear you," when I asked for a cappuccino, but I wasn't even asking him. I was asking Dirk since he was treating me, as I made the goddamn dinner in the first place.

Apparently, I have no patience with anyone these days, and I snap at them for no good reason at all, and I insist it isn't my medication, but some assholes beg to differ. I think it is a general irritation in the air affecting a lot of people because there is so much shit in the news these days, from Ebola to war to men not respecting women and being complete dick-brains.

As we left the counter with our coffees and desserts, I told the server I was an old tart and Dirk was a young tart—we demolished our butter tarts with two huge bites before we even got to the table—but he didn't bother to respond. He was the only server on duty that night and didn't seem to know enough to put on music, so the coffee shop had this quiet eerie feeling like it was the end of the world, and it made both me and Dirk feel very bleak and light-hearted and prompted us to make very questionable remarks to each other.

Anyway, after we ate our tarts, Dirk told me, as we passed Loblaws, that he thought that once some dealer sold him sidewalk salt instead of crystal meth. And then a few blocks later, after we hadn't talked for at least four and a half minutes, he said, "sidewalk salt can look a lot like meth," and I said, "yeah, it can, and cat grass can look a lot like chives."

I did actually once serve cat grass to a friend, on pasta, and I thought it tasted kind of bland, but he immediately identified it as cat grass. He kind of looked like a very skinny, bald Abraham Lincoln, and I had a huge crush on him for as long as it took to eat that cat grass pasta with a lovely side salad that had no animal-intended foodstuffs on it as far as I know. I sometimes see the Abraham Lincoln look-a-like on Church Street, but I turn away so he won't notice me because I am never in the mood any longer to fall in love with people who look like dead presidents.

At one point, Dirk mentioned bodily excretions coming from the same place, and I had to remind him that the gods gave us two places for those very separate waste products to leave our bodies from. I think he got confused because of the cat grass/chives mix-up, but I'm not completely sure. We were both a little high from the butter tarts and the cappuccinos and were just yakking away at each other a mile a minute, making very little sense in the grand scheme of things. And then we saw a stray dog raise its leg on the gay village rainbow sign, and that made us laugh and feel a bit sick at the same time. Needless to say, cats and dogs do a lot of things with their tongues in close proximity to the places from which they urinate and defecate, so that was maybe what prompted Dirk to make that rather odd comment about where numbers one and two come from. Who knows? Dirk is a very sweet guy—when he says peculiar things, I know it is not because he means them. He just has a very comical, abject way of looking at the world, like I do, and it makes us think very offbeat, vulgar things on a regular basis. And if you say weird things enough, sometimes you start to believe them.

I told Dirk about how I once wrote a piece of creative non-fiction based on a real-life experience. That's what I hate about creative non-fiction—it has to be based on an actual experience. I prefer fictional memoir myself. I wrote this piece about a guy on the gulf coast of Florida who took me to his place on an island with a causeway. After sleeping with him at his lovely little bunga-low on Key Lime Drive, I decided to rename the island Sani-flush, which actually sounds a lot like the actual name of the place. He had furniture covered in tiny seashells, and he was into, well, eating you-know-what. It kind of grossed me out, and I kept thinking of the old jokes about Sweet Marie chocolate bars, but when I actually saw a bit of it in the corner of his mouth, I thought to myself, 'Well, this is definitely the beginning and the end of my little experience with anyone who likes to eat you-know-what out of someone's you-know-where.' I am not judging his little habit, but it is not one of my chosen fetishes—and given my current condi-tion, it probably would not be the healthiest choice as far as extracurricular social activities go.

I got that piece of creative non-fiction published in a sex journal in New York, and I used a fake name. That was a require-ment invented by the publisher—he told me that famous writers had done the same thing. They had written about real-life experiences that kind of require a fake name if you have any intention of keeping your dignity and not letting people know that sometimes ordinary people take part in what some may consider very unappetizing situations. I happen to be currently reading a collection of fictionalized memoir pieces by one of those famous writers who once asked me at a book-signing if it was okay to embellish the truth in your writing. I had told him I was a writer too, so I think that's what prompted him to ask me. I told him that of course it was, because no one really remembers what actually happened anyway, and that the old adage is in fact a bold-faced lie—the truth is not always stranger than fiction. Sometimes the truth is just plain boring and needs a little spice to make it tastier. He seemed to like my answer a lot, and when we parted company, he began to chat personably with another complete stranger who wanted him to sign their goddamn book. I could never be a famous author because I would end up swearing at people at book-signings and making rude comments, all the time expecting them to understand that I just have a very offbeat, vulgar sense of humour that only people like Dirk get a kick out of.

I used to get obsessed with celebrities and think they should instantly take me into their lives when I meet them at book-signings and other public events. I got over that very quickly after a couple of extremely embarrassing encounters where the authorities had to be brought in, and a certain amount of shouting and forced restraint became necessary. But I still sometimes think to myself that the famous writer at the book-signing must think about me from time to time and regret not adopting me, even though I am a few years older than him, and his long-time partner might not be into it. I could cook and clean for them, and edit his creative non-fiction for a paltry fee, and help him turn it into something a little less truthful and a great deal more interesting than the reading public might be expecting from a well-known semi-memoirist.

Dirk and I are both pissed off at our mutual, unpublished, creative non-fiction, writer friend Hedwig for different reasons. I've obviously changed his name to Hedwig to protect his total lack of innocence. I'm pissed off because Hedwig told me my meds were poison, and when I told him that I just followed doctor's or-

ders and that they were very beneficial considering my condition, Hedwig just looked at me with his precious, holier-than-thou, condescending, bullshit look and said—all sad and precious—"Is that what they told you?" with a condescending quiver in his voice and such a fucking sad smile just trembling on the edge of his fucking new-age-lip-service lips. And I just wanted to say back to him, "No, they told me to just lie down and die and inject myself with gallons of fresh ginger and tofu and gluten-free cat shit, and that would give me unbearable but profoundly healing heartburn and also cause me to miraculously levitate and be instantly cured of the gateway pathology to the gay fucking plague, and then I would be free of the evil poisonous medicine being ruthlessly pedalled (according to Hedwig) by the demonic medical profession hell-bent on selling us cat grass instead of chives and sidewalk salt instead of meth and putting shit in our mouths under the guise of healing us with anti-retroviral drugs that are the conspiracy of huge pharmaceutical corporations killing Africa and half the sick world at a huge profit for themselves and their loved ones!"
Hedwig does have a point but tends to go way too far with it, when in fact I am just trying to live and thoroughly enjoy what's left of my goddamn life in peace, and I don't have time to be a writer of heavily embellished creative non-fiction, as well as someone who searches for every single goddamn holistic cure for HIV and AIDS!

Dirk is pissed off at Hedwig because he told him he should do everything he does as a recovering addict. I told Dirk to tell Hedwig that if he did that he would disappear inside his own asshole, and we both laughed and agreed that might not be the best way to handle things. So instead of telling Hedwig what we thought, we both just decided to see less of him. Which is kind of sad because we both love him so much and wish him well. Hedwig has been a huge support to both of us in troubled times, but when Dirk said goodnight, I knew there was this unspoken agreement between us that loving people can sometimes be marketed as a very positive thing when in fact it just turns to shit as soon as they start talking, giving advice, and just being all-around mouthy assholes, kind of like me and Dirk. But we do it in private.

Dirk is pushing thirty and I am pushing sixty, so he is half my age, which is just plain annoying and demeaning, but ours is a perfectly lovely example of an inter-generational friendship where two people have experienced similar things in their lives three decades apart. Ain't life grand. That's what I always fucking say: Ain't life grand! I was never a drug addict, not for lack of trying, but I was a poorly-paid hooker for about three hours, and the trick just stuck a twenty in my ski mitt and went home to the suburbs. My roommate at the time told me I was smart to take him to our place because he was more apt to kill me if I went to his place. I didn't really understand the rationale behind that, and it turned out he was totally non-violent and all I did was jerk him off. He didn't even take off his pants. We met in the lobby of the Royal York Hotel. It was the nineteen-seventies—I was wearing russet platform shoes, beige bell-bottom dress pants, and a brown velvet dinner jacket. My hair was natural blonde and parted in the centre, and I perhaps looked like an expensive young hooker at the time even though that was not my intention when I dressed for the evening.

Dirk is coming over again tomorrow for dinner because he loved the baked potato so much I promised to make him another one right away—he said he would be over tomorrow at seven. It is way too soon to make dinner for him again, but—what the hell—we get along pretty well, and after the second baked potato, I probably won't see him again for a few weeks. He's very popular. I think I will put cat grass on the potato and see if he notices. I hope I don't run into Abraham Lincoln on the way to the pet shop. Despite my best intentions, I might fall for him all over again.

Loblaws

It was a day like any other day, inspiring sentences like so many other sentences. Nothing original about it. In fact, if one were to adopt a literary model, it could be argued—successfully—that the day had stolen all of its best lines from so many other days. But I still got up out of bed, against my better judgment, and remembered how to put on my clothes as I began to prepare for whatever life had borrowed from other lives for me to experience over the course of the next thirteen installments of sixty-minute intervals all designed to lend order to our chaotic lives.

It was 11:00 a.m. Almost half the day was gone. What a difference that makes to twenty-four little hours, to cut them in half and spare one's self the luminescent glare of another goddamn sunny morning. I like to keep my sunglasses on the bedside table just in case the curtains have accidentally been left open and I am wakened by the unpredictable energy of my least favourite planet. I know that the sun is a star, but I prefer to think of it as a misunderstood planet for exiled malcontents to wander around, fiery and filled with rage for everything that crosses their interstellar paths.

As I dress each morning, I am reminded of how forgetting how to put on one's clothes has been something that has haunted me ever since I witnessed an elderly gentleman—in the nursing home where my mother lived—struggling to put on his sweater. He seemed much too distressed and angry for a stranger to approach him. At one point, he had the armhole over his head. It was kind of an interesting look, like Garbo in *Ninotchka* with a seamless opalescent veil. I was about to offer assistance when a nurse came to his rescue. My mother nonchalantly looked at me and said, "He's from the third floor, the Old Timers' ward." She always said *Old Timers'* instead of *Alzheimer's* after hearing someone refer to it that way in a TV movie. I had come over to take her for pizza. She loved pizza, and it was a welcome change from the nursing home food she hated but I loved. I always finished her meals for her.

So that morning, like any other morning, I got out of bed, self-consciously dressed myself, and boiled an egg. My roommate's leftover pizza in the fridge acted as an appetizer before the egg was ready. A small crystal juice glass, half filled with Prosecco, and the other half filled with a pulpy fruit medley, helped to wash down my elegant impromptu late-morning snack. There had been a faintly sexual and undesignated celebration the evening before in my roommate's bedroom, and some booze had found its way into one of my favourite heirloom tumblers—just the right size to act as a juice glass. I had poured it before going to bed, after leaving my voluptuous tenant's room, so I would have a little libational pick-me-up when I awoke. Champagne and fruit juice at home always make me feel like I'm still in my early thirties and living in an expensive hotel. My sexuality is like that fictionalized river Margaret Laurence talks about in *The Diviners*. It runs both ways.

I dressed quickly, in case I suddenly forgot how to put on socks or underwear part way through, or when exactly to put them on. I have an irrational fear of leaving the house one day without realizing that I have slipped my underwear on over my trousers, or my head.

Ceci n'est pas un chapeau.

So I dressed at breakneck speed, had breakfast, put on my hat and coat, and went out to greet the day with the silent bravado of an aging diva hell bent on remembering how to remain calm in a volcanic world. As I got off the elevator, I looked at the bulletin board in the lobby and let out a little squeal.

"Shit. Not today. I hate those fucking members' meetings."

I only went for the pizza and the armed police officer. I don't like guns, but I love a handsome, strapping holster. There is just something about all that bulk, the tight, heavily packed uniform and the ambient bulges here and there with the little Velcro or domed flaps concealing whatever it is they carry in those little pockets placed strategically all over their uniforms. The decision to have an armed police officer present at every members' meeting had been made by the board of directors after a violent altercation between two warring residents who actually stopped an elevator once long enough to have a fist fight. It seemed to be the only place on the premises where their outbursts would go uninterrupted, at least for as long as it took the fire department to arrive. What on earth would a firefighter do? Spray them? But that seemed to be the order of the day when someone was trapped, voluntarily or otherwise, on an elevator in the co-op where I live. In the excitable meeting that prompted the board to hire police officers, the resident offenders just slapped each other and cried out in elevated tones, like good fags do, and stormed out of the room. I often wondered whether they took separate lifts back to their apartments or got in the same one and just kept slapping all the way up. They both lived at the top of the building, in side-by-side units, one of which had been raided when a former tenant was found to have firearms. Apparently, he threw a small, loaded pistol into the street from his balcony when the police broke down the door. He was evicted soon after, and many residents were very angry with the board of directors due to the fact that he had even been allowed to live there in the first place. All I could think was, 'It must be very hard to design applications and interview procedures where you can find out for sure whether or not the future tenant might ever be in possession of an illegal weapon. Should they be frisked before they sign the housing contract or should every co-op be equipped with a body scanner at the doorway?'

The board had also decided to offer free pizza and soda pop

at members' meetings, and there was always a raffle for a grocery gift card at the end of the meeting. This was done in order to attract more people and raise numbers to a level that would provide a quorum and the continuation of meetings designed to pass budgets and other pressing items on any given agenda. The idea for gift cards was initially resisted because of the complex raffle system that might lead to theft, mayhem, and attempted murder. But one night, an especially adventurous quorum voted it in.

This particular co-op members' meeting was happening at an especially inconvenient time. I had forgotten to jot it down in my daybook and had made plans to go with a friend to a late-afternoon film that would end only ten minutes before the meeting started. The leftover Prosecco in my water bottle, which I had stolen from the half empty bottle my roommate had left in the bathroom sink, would be delightful with buttered popcorn during the film, but would ultimately exhaust me by the time I got back to the co-op. But at the end of the day, all things considered, free pizza was not something I could pass up on my limited budget. So I would rush home and go to the meeting, a little boozed up but perhaps not noticeably so.

At the end of the film, a ninety-minute romantic comedy about an eighty-year-old American lesbian couple fleeing homophobic idiocy to get married in Canada, I went to Loblaws—formerly known as Maple Leaf Gardens—with my film companion. In the produce section, close to where the stage might have been when it was a multi-purpose arena, I was filled with star-studded memories, and began an interminable monologue that my friend endured by squeezing grapefruits, oranges, and sundry items.

"When I saw Frank Sinatra here, he was so out of it, he couldn't even follow the lyrics on the monitor, and he made xenophobic remarks about Kurt Weill's name when he sang *Mack the Knife*, followed by some insipid comment about Richard Rodgers and the great American songbook. Moron! Did he even know anything about Rodgers' German Jewish heritage, that his original surname was Abrahams, changed by his father, a prominent surgeon in Queen's, and that Lorenz Hart, one of Rodgers' greatest collaborators, was a lovesick homosexual who was obsessed with Desi Arnaz and stood up for him when he married Lucille Ball? But I forgot about all the weird shit going on onstage when Frank sang *My Way*. I just cried. It was so beautiful, even though he did seem a little unsure of the lyrics. And Steve Lawrence and Eydie Gormé opened for Frank, and she was in such a bad mood. I could have sworn she was drunk the way she lugged herself across the stage in some horrific watercolour chiffon caftan and said such snippy things to Steve. I always loved Steve, and Eydie, but she was so off that night. And when I saw Freddy Mercury here, I had no idea who he was. A friend made me go to see his favourite new band named Queen, and I thought it was such a weird name for a rock band, but I went because I had such a crush on that friend, even though he was straight, and dating my best girlfriend, and he kind of looked like Freddy, and had a very sexy moustache and large manly breasts in high school, so I couldn't resist. And Linda Ronstadt— she said, during the concert, in between songs, that she was going to sing another Elvis song after singing *Love Me Tender*, and I was so disappointed it was *Alison* by Elvis Costello and not *Jailhouse Rock* or *Burning Love*."

As I finished blathering on about Frank, Eydie, Elvis, Linda, and Freddy, I noticed frozen pizza with roasted garlic and asiago cheese on sale for $2.99. So I stuffed four into the shopping cart and felt very pleased with the bargain, half forgetting I had already eaten leftover pizza for breakfast and that there would still be lots more to consume when I got home.

All in all, it was a delightful visit to Loblaws, the former home of Canada's greatest pastime, hockey, and countless summer concerts when the ice was gone and the stage was set for touring acts from all over the world. The sordid memory of much-publicized tales of abuse inflicted upon young hockey players at the hands of older sports enthusiasts, always made me very sad as I looked at the site of an old entrance that had once had emblazoned across the door *Equipment Handling Room.*

Halfway back to my apartment, I remembered the co-op meeting. I was strolling slowly, a little worn out from the Prosecco during the movie, and had completely forgotten about it. I began to walk much faster and got there about ten minutes after it had started. And there they were, six large boxes filled with pizza—one Hawaiian, two pepperoni and cheese, one vegetarian, and two tomato, feta, and mozzarella—with cans of Ginger Ale, Coke, Diet Pepsi, Seven-Up, and some kind of carbonated cranberry drink. Wandering through Loblaws, overwhelmed by the bittersweet cinematic romance of an aging lesbian couple, I had forgotten about the pizza that would be available at the meeting. Now I had four frozen ones in my bag that would be half-thawed by the time the meeting ended. As much as I loved it, pizza was going to be an unwelcome staple of my diet for the rest of the week.

I sat there, filled with popcorn and sparkling wine, in the co-op meeting room, trying not to stare at the beautiful, bulky, lesbian police officer. I shouldn't have, but just assumed she was lesbian because she was a police officer and very butch. She probably had four kids and a cute, skinny house husband at home for all I knew. But there she stood, instead of the muscular, tightly-packed police officer of the biological male persuasion. I wasn't really all that disappointed. My faint but notable bisexual tendencies were given a little airtime and I settled into an unexpected bout of voyeurism while the rest of the room ate their pizza and listened to a lot of boring shit about budgets and how to discipline your pet when in public areas in and around the co-op, especially on the elevator, where house pets can really pose a problem for anyone terrified of being bitten, or worse, pissed on in confined spaces. And then, for some inexplicable reason, as I caught the eye of the woman police officer, I quickly looked away and then down at my trousers to make sure I wasn't wearing underwear over them, and then I lightly grazed the side of my head with my left palm to make sure I didn't have panties on instead of a hat. Lucky for me, I wasn't. That would have been very embarrassing. And as I stared at my pants, straightened my customary cap, and reached for a slice of Hawaiian on the table beside me, I thanked god for the serenity to accept the things I cannot change. In my muddled mood, I also suddenly remembered a performance I had seen by an ex-porn star, Annie Sprinkle, where she asked for an audience member to take her panties off for her before she did a procedure with a speculum where she let spectators look at her cervix with a flashlight. I raised my hand, ran up, carefully slipped off her black lace undies with the pearl below the navel, then slipped them over my own trousers, and pranced back to my seat. It was an exciting night in my life that I will never forget—well, so long as I don't get Alzheimer's. But sometimes people with Alzheimer's do inexplicable things, like wearing a pair of treasured underwear over their trousers for no apparent reason, even though deep in their brain, the memory of an especially exciting night of live performance could be imbedded. I also have a photo of Annie with her right breast on my head and her left breast on my lesbian friend's head. She was selling the pictures for five dollars after the show.

After the members' meeting, that night, like any other night, I readied myself for bed, washing my face and brushing my teeth, things I often felt too tired to do but always tried to force on myself—at least the teeth, since the face isn't a priority in the area of health insurance. If the face goes, Social Services definitely won't help. If the teeth go, they will give a bit of assistance. As I readied myself for bed, I began to mutter the Serenity Prayer under my breath:

> *I thank God for the small but beautiful way*
> *in which alcohol has touched my life today.*

And then, of course, I instantly reminded myself that this was not the Serenity Prayer. It was my serenity prayer. I had written it in response to an Al-Anon meeting where one of the participants became enraged that no one seemed interested in listening to her longwinded diatribe about a philandering lover. It just wasn't her turn to speak, but that didn't seem to be an organizing principle that she had any time for. So she stormed out, leaving a sublime scent of booze behind her. One couldn't help but wonder whether she had mistaken herself for someone profoundly affected by the behaviour of alcoholics rather than an alcoholic herself.* But that would be one of her many life missions, not mine. I knew who I was and was grasping memories tightly for as I long as I possibly could.

That night, like so many nights, I put my thoughts to rest with the proper version of the Serenity Prayer and went to sleep. It had been a day like any other day, except, of course, for the abundance of pizza.

*Al-Anon and AA are not the same thing even though they do torture the same vowel that opens the drunken alphabet.

Canlit, and other Cunning Linguists

Try to feel, in your heart's core, the reality of others.
This is the most painful thing in the world, probably,
and the most necessary.
     —Margaret Laurence

My mother used to tell me, when I was a bit older,
that the secret of a successful marriage
was to sleep in a double bed.
     —Xaviera Hollander

People parted, years passed, they met again—and the
meeting proved no reunion, offered no warm memories,
only the acid knowledge that time had passed
and things weren't as bright or attractive
as they had been.
     —Jacqueline Susann

We cannot tear out a single page of our life,
but we can throw the whole book in the fire.
     —George Sand

A woman has to live her life, or live to repent not having lived it...
We've got to live, no matter how many skies have fallen.
     —D.H. Lawrence, *Lady Chatterley's Lover*

Dear Margaret,

Please stop following me! I first started to notice your writing when my Nana came home from church that day in 1976 after reading excerpts from your banned book laid bare on some gilded, righteous, pompous pulpit, highlighted in the foyer beside the donation box. She agreed with townsfolk who had saddened you, comparing your work to Jacqueline Susann and Xaviera Hollander. I should be so lucky, Margaret, I should be so lucky.

I stopped myself from telling Nana that Ms. Hollander's *The Happy Hooker*, Ms. Susann's *Valley of the Dolls*, and Mr. Lawrence's *Lady Chatterley's Lover* were hidden under packets of Kleenex in the night table drawers, dog-eared and devoured, in my parents' bedroom in my early teens when I would sneak in and flip wildly through the pages for descriptions of sex. But there was no sign of your pages, Margaret, in our house—just popular novels, pocket westerns, movie magazines, and sensational bestsellers I adored, but I loved yours too as you laid bare the stories of our lives. The stories you told, they lived with me long before I read them.

Nana just rambled on indignantly and told me she had dropped a dime into the Plexiglas box to support the good work of the church. She had been so immersed in those yellowed stanzas set apart by fluorescent, felt-tipped, thought police. She read your banned words for too long and missed the tea party in the church basement. She had been so looking forward to those fresh strawberry tarts and that odd but tantalizing herbal tea she had never tasted in her youth. She told me that she could never have imagined tea without milk and sugar—so refreshing, so daring, so wild, with exotic names like Jasmine, Elderberry, and Sleepy Time, and she always loved to pronounce herbal with a voiced "h."

Upon leaving the church she went straight to a bookstore, bought a copy of *The Diviners*, read it from cover to cover, by the end seething strongly enough to feel the need to proclaim to her adolescent grandson, in hushed, enraged tones, "She must have a very dirty mind to be able to think up all those vulgar things she writes about."

I grew up immersed in Nana's songs and stories, haunted by my gradual disbelief in everything she sang and told, from songs of lady mice marrying gentleman frogs to tales providing puritan titillation and righteous indignation. I was enchanted by the quiet flow of her tender fervour, coming to believe that finally stories are just the things we tell ourselves to make up lives to lead and listen to, inventing new narratives to thrill us and keep us safe from things that should never frighten us. Now I spend my life in stories I have told and told and told.

I was fifteen, Margaret, when you began to write *The Diviners*, and I rode along that tarnished misidentified river you made iconic with your words and the thoughts of all I desired that I would never speak of for almost a decade, and then never stop speaking of for the rest of my life.

The river flowed both ways.
The current moved from north to south, but the wind
usually came from the south, rippling the bronze-green
water in the opposite direction. This apparently
impossible contradiction, made apparent and possible,
still fascinated Morag, even after the years of river-watching.

I leapt from ravaged cliffs, swung from knotted ropes strung from swaying bark-bent trees into that tamed river like the strong brown god of T.S. Eliot's intractable flow. The river mimicked my body's writhing and the beautiful braying glow of light, skin-darkening sun, rippling waves of coursing flesh moving both ways in and out of love with the skin of strangers. As light traced the cancer-teasing tan-lines of former summers, the morning air in a small provincial town, once school had ended, lured my bored and girlish frame into those rays as I rode and rode and rode along that beautiful river's edge looking for something I suspected I might find in the water or the trees, something that was never there, something that I never found, always on the horizon but never touched.

Growing so tired of all that beauty, the atmosphere of spent adolescence, lifting and heaving in my denim cutoffs like the steamy sentences of Xaveria Hollander's exposés, my shorts created the syntax of purple prose and soapy fiction in the low-lying literary caverns of my wordy thighs, anxiously awaiting another summer visit from him and his family.

To live and write, to revisit the wild and filthy vulgar violet vim and busty beauty of cheap priceless words, whispered into our ears by our loved ones' unconditional contradictions, then to leave it all behind us like a faded, pulsing scar only to come back again to say

> *I couldn't care less who I did it with, even my relatives.*
> *In fact, the idea of sampling forbidden fruit*
> *made incest all the more exciting.*
> *The only taboo against it was*
> *we don't make babies, that's all.*
> —Xaviera Hollander, *The Happy Hooker*

But Nana ranted, rambled on, unaware of stories her lineage was telling and retelling, her solid ravings resistant, raucous music to my ears about to take her words so I could rage against them long after she was gone. "I'm glad they've banned her book from the schools because you can't be reading about that sort of thing at such a tender age."

Having felt so little tenderness at any age, immersed by generation upon generation of family horror, my Nana's shady innocence fell on numb ears.

I remember your heroines, Margaret, like I remember loneliness—something to gravitate toward as respite from the frightening solidarity of conditional love, learning to long for self-enforced estrangement more than any therapist in their right mind might condone.

Love shouldn't make a beggar of one.
I wouldn't want love if I had to beg for it, to barter or qualify it.
And I should despise it if anyone ever begged for my love.
Love is something that must be given—
it can't be bought with words or pity, or even reason.
—Jacqueline Susann, Valley of the Dolls

And then, Margaret, I found your Perfume Sea, seeing myself in Mr. Archipelago's queer spaces as he slid swiftly sliding fingers slipping softly through fond folded silken threads of saris baked in fragrant tumid rooms. Half in love with your dreams of Africa, I fell headlong into euphuistic lyric glades of alliteration, sounding words like stolen blood-dappled diamonds, grafting themselves upon the gorgeous golden hair of younger arms, glistening much like my own back then in glory's daze.

At twenty, wandering blind to love from Tangier to Marrakech at the mercy of my well-kept lie of blonde chaste purity, protected by nothing but fresh memories of welcome trauma bubbling in my eyes—and the worried eyes of tall, straight protectors who saw breathtaking girlishness barely fading in my face and thighs. They kept me from all the harm I gravitated toward. I would have loved them to lie down upon my cries, suffocating in their puerile sexless aid. I had to steal away from long, platonic limbs into the Medina on the backs of strangers' motorbikes, trading clothes from Le Chateau for a still-warm teapot scented with the mint of his mother's tea leaves. He called it silver brass. We sat side by side on his modest bed, watched the screen of a huge colour TV flash images bleeding beads of light into the corners of an autographed photo of Susannah York sitting on top of the television set.

And then he rode me back like some willful Tess on a moped to that cheap hotel where my concerned travelling companions scolded me for bold and careless journeys. I had this flash of you, Margaret, then, in my self-willed, wild heart—you're still there, I've let you wallow, please stop following me. I have loved being followed.

> *Women, as well as men, in all ages and in all places,*
> *have danced on the earth, danced the life dance,*
> *danced joy, danced grief, danced despair, and danced hope.*
> *Literally and metaphorically, by their very lives.*
> —Margaret Laurence, *Dance on the Earth: a Memoir*

But now I'm old, and happy to be old, as your writing still tracks my every move in narrative that enfolds me. I have kept that early eighties' photo of you shaking my hand at twenty-four, you in your chancellor's gown, me in my trendy plastic shoes.

Lithe, pleated, pale-grey, dove-like trousers; my full, blond wedge at graduation. I read so much into that fleeting snapshot meeting—your knowing smile that carries me on verbose wings through these clichéd stanzas, worlds of love for people and the objects we adore and covet as bodies and emotions fail us.

Now, in a century you never inhabited but in which you have given so much to those of us moving through the organized mess of faintly nurturant late-capitalist madness, having lived in a downtown co-op named after you, for twenty years, half imagining a large, framed black and white print of us as a photographic homage in the foyer encased within Plexiglas boxes alongside your pages folded back, highlighted in pink felt-tipped fury.

How I never fought for anything here among these sanitized corridors of barely-affordable housing until well-meaning misguided zealots tried to take your name away from this threatened haven I have treasured for so long. They pleaded, with the pithy aid of PowerPoint plotting, in the classist name of "We don't want the stigma of living in a government-subsidized building, so let's just change the sign, and we can tell that famous lady writer she can have a plaque in the lobby."

But on the banks of currents I was weaned on running every which way, back and forth through treacherous, taming locks on stolen land with bridges, fields, and mangled lakes, there you were, blessing my life for so long in the pages, the church foyers, and the minds of beloved maternal grandmothers hell-bent on ingesting your gorgeous garishness, then brandishing it unfit.

It's all behind us now, so please stop following me, Margaret; rest, find the places that the people you created never found; rest, I can carry what is left of me from here to there; rest, stop following me; rest, you have given everything I need, to rest…xo

When I thought I was a Mango

Just a spoonful of sugar helps the medicine go down
in a most delightful way.
    —Mary Poppins

I ponder and I cannot ponder, yet I live and love.
    —William Blake

On a warm sunny Wednesday in March, when the weather suited global warming to a tee, he took his small shopping buggy from the balcony and set out for the food bank. Only a few blocks from his apartment, this particular food bank specialized in healthy items that came in containers ranging from plastic freezer airtight bags to small meat-bearing styrofoam platters, cardboard boxes, foil wrappers, and glass jars.

He always looked forward to eating the two or three miniature granola bars on his way home, after judiciously making his selection of mostly non-perishable goods. He always marvelled at how something that appeared to be so nutritious—Nature's Choice—could come in such a shiny, unnatural-looking wrapper. If he saved enough of them, he could turn them inside out and cover his bathroom wall with a glistening silver coating and then hang pictures of celebrities all over the wall, turning his latrine into a modest shrine for the silver screen.

In the waiting area at the food bank, there was always a

transparent, dome-covered plastic tray filled with hot cross buns, danishes, brownies, cinnamon wedges, butter tarts, and assorted donuts of the delicious kind. They were all cut into bite-sized portions and had a crumbling nostalgic air about them that spoke of slightly better days. But they were delicious. There were metal prongs and napkins to keep the delicacies safe from germ warfare, and a large canister of hot coffee sat on a table nearby, with powdered milk and a box of sugar to help the medicine go down.

He put his buggy beside his chair and went over to the reception desk to check in. Stating his name and answering one simple question was always enough. They never asked for ID because he had registered several years ago and was in the computer system. They trusted him. But he always took ID with him just in case. One would not want to be caught with their pants down and no conceivable way of identifying one's self in such a welcoming atmosphere. The pants-down metaphor seemed appropriate because he, and perhaps some others, were only eligible for this particular food bank because they had, through no fault of their own, been caught with their trousers to the floor one too many times.

The simple question the receptionist always asked was: "Do you have any pets?" He would pause for a second, considering what he might do with the jars of cat food or doggy kibble. Perhaps he could sell them, or mix them with a rich salty stew that would conceal their true identity? And then he would think better of his thrifty capitalist ways and reply, "No. But thank you."

Then he would take one or two selections from the pastry tray, fill a styrofoam cup with coffee, add some powdered milk and a touch of sugar, and sit back down to wait until his fruit or vegetable was called. It wasn't a long wait, and the variety of colourful, laminated fruit and veggie bearing cards made it fun:

Apple
Banana
Blackberry
Cantaloupe
Date
Fennel
Ginger
Jalapeño
Kiwi
Lime
Mango
Okra
Peach
Pumpkin
Radicchio
Yam
Zucchini

He would often arrive shortly after 2:00 p.m. The food bank was open from 2:00 until 7:00 p.m. By the time he arrived, they would be as far along as Cantaloupes. He would receive a Fennels laminated card and wait until his group of three or four was called. Once, when he arrived earlier than usual, he was a Date, and knew that the usual gag would be played as soon as the Dates were called.

"Dates anyone? Any Dates?"
Inevitably someone would laugh and say something along the lines of, "I'd love to. Haven't been on a date in ages."

But on this particularly warm Wednesday in March, he arrived well after two, missed the Dates, and thought he was a Mango. He took his card, walked over to his chair, sat down and saw a familiar face in a wheelchair. Noticing that his close acquaintance also had a Mango card, he said, "I've never been a Mango before. I'm usually a Fennel." His friend smiled but said nothing. Apart from the Dates, not much was made of the other fruits and vegetables in the area of small talk. So he just sat—

sipping coffee and nibbling at the ragged corner of a hot cross bun—and waited for the Mangoes to to be herded down to the selection area.

Consumed by a commingling of good cheer and slight melancholy—a mixture of emotion that invariably held him somewhere between a subtle smile and a face that was holding back tears—he noticed that the attendant who was passing out the laminated cards looked quite agitated. He could overhear him explaining to an assistant that the fruit and vegetable cards were all mixed up, and that he was sending down the groups in all the wrong order.

How hard could it be to have noticed that, he thought, and just sort them properly, in alphabetical order. But it wasn't his place to make any sort of suggestion as to how organizing principles might be applied in such a setting. So he sat patiently, watching the names of each fruit or vegetable come and go on the pixel board above the reception desk—in the wrong order—wondering anxiously if his Mango would ever come up.

After several minutes had passed, he went up to the desk and politely asked if his fruit had risen. The confused receptionist asked what fruit he was and, when he said Mango, he told him to go ahead —the Mangoes had already been called. So he left the reception area and walked briskly toward the stairwell of the food bank. On his way, he saw the assistant who had been taking the groups down the stairs to the area where the shelves of dry goods and freezers filled with assorted frozen meats were kept. He looked at him, smiled, and said—"I think the fruits and vegetables got a little mixed up today. I was told to go ahead." The assistant looked at his card and said, politely but somewhat abruptly—"No. I'll call you when it's time."

A little bewildered, he walked back to the waiting area—and waited. As he sat, for about five minutes, he kept looking at the pixel board and could not make head nor tail of how things were being reorganized. The mangoes had already gone and the order seemed to have been reestablished on the pixel board. And then, after several seconds of low-level anxiety marked by his signature tendency to fluctuate between a faint smile and suppressed tears, he looked at his laminated card, and much to his surprise, and embarrassment, he was not a Mango at all. He was a Pumpkin. Cinderella immediately popped into his mind with the change from M to P. Suppressing images of little white mice sewing spectacular gowns and singing bibbidy- bobbidy-boo, he made a quick decision not to dwell upon the clichéd, fairy-tale proportions of the mix-up. Instead, he sat and waited patiently until the Pumpkins were called, during which time he pondered, until he could not ponder, how this could have happened. He was certain he had been a Mango. And then, at the height of his low-level anxiety, he looked at the camera option on his cell phone, remembering that he had taken a photo of his card soon after arriving, so he could write a little story about this particular food bank one day—about the delightful and efficient alphabetical manner in which they organized their patrons into groups of fruits and vegetables.

Yes, indeed. Cameras seldom lie. He had always been a Pumpkin, and when he chatted with the close acquaintance in the wheelchair, and noticed that his card said Mango, he must have simply assumed he was one too because the colours of the cards depicting the very different fruits were so similar.

It all made perfect sense, because he knew, in his heart, he had always been a princess. So it seemed fitting, after all this time—some sixty-odd years—that he would one day find himself, at the PWA food bank (strictly serving a community of people living with HIV and AIDS) abruptly turning back into a Pumpkin.

Testicles, Ten Bricks,
and a Tumour

"It isn't the cough that carries you off,
it's the coffin they carry you off in."
        —unidentified old saying my father often told me

It was a story his father told him. He took it to heart. I always felt he was born a bit of an idiot savant. He had an enormous capacity to learn but no real way of retaining all of the relatively useless knowledge he chose to take in. Also, he would type words like *retain* and it would always come out *retina*. Every time he wrote an essay, he had to check for all the typos where he would consistently key in *from* instead of *form*: inevitably, *performance* came out *perfromance*. He was very smart about just how stupid he was capable of being. As he got older, he grew fond of saying, about himself, "I know almost nothing about absolutely everything." The vast amount of information he did take in, well, it seemed to be constantly leaking out of his brain but leaving an indelible trace of the factual that he somehow muddled into the most astonishing and outlandish fictional beliefs. He kept them a secret, for the most part, but told me a few as we lay in bed late at night, in our early teens, and then once every decade after that, into our sixties. He would summon me, and I'd be there. We were always in touch but only met once in a blue moon. Just lying together and telling each other unbelievable stories, but wishing we had kept our mouths shut, had rolled on top of one another, and had our way the moment the inclination hit us. But we never did. We just told tales—tall ones, laced with a sizeable amount of non-fiction.

At seven years old, that one formative story came to him through his father's distorted gaze, on a hot summer afternoon just after he had taken a shit in the outhouse just up the hill behind the cottage, lined in front with a bed of poppies in full bloom, and in back with scrawny poplars hung with plastic lemons. His dad was standing outside, peering into the narrow slit of a crescent-moon-shaped hole carved into the upper portion of the makeshift lavatory door, trying to tell his son how to properly wipe his own ass.

"Don't waste paper. I'll be long gone, but the day will come when rolls of ass-wipe and boat loads of water for the indoor latrines will be few and far between. Be frugal, you little bastard, or I'll wipe your skinny crack with sandpaper. That'll teach ya. Now take two squares, fold them carefully after the first wipe, and then again for every other wipe you need. Don't use more than that unless it's a really big dump. And just flush once!" But he never learned. On his own, he once told me, without his father at the door, he always spun off several squares and crumpled them, ball-like, into the designated orifice, maybe used it once more, then took another hand full until he felt his ass had been thoroughly and gently scoured, and then he would flush, several times, to get rid of all the excess tissue.

But that wasn't the full story, just the preamble. One of the many times his father tried to educate him regarding the proper use of toilet tissue, he let out a little shriek as he was wiping. "What's the matter kiddo? You sound like a sissy. Did a bullfrog bite your balls in there? What's up? Get yer butt clean and get outta there. It's a great day for bananafish out here in the sun. Yer cousins are all down by the lake soakin' up the rays gettin' skin cancer and havin' a wail of a time. Get your little white ass down there, Boy!"

He had caught his left testicle between the rough wooden

edge of the outhouse hole—cut irregularly, a distorted oval, into the wood of the overall seating structure—and the porcelain toilet seat screwed loosely into the wood. As he tried to follow his father's impatiently-plotted instructions, he had fidgeted and squirmed one too many times and the seat slid sideways as he wiped, throwing one nut inadvertently into precisely the wrong place at precisely the wrong time. He was young enough then to have no pubic hair to speak of, thereby saving him the added agony of delicate neophyte hairs being pulled from the wrinkly folds of his youthful nut sac. But significant damage to one square inch of pre-pubescent tissue did leave a scar and produced enough blood to choke a toad. His shriek turned into a cry as his father pulled the door open, breaking the little latch from the wall. He grabbed his son from the seat, cradled him in his arms, pants still down to his nine year old ward's skinny ankles, and immediately sussing out the unseemly predicament, rushed down to the lake in full view of several faintly inbred cousins frolicking by the beach.

"Get outta here kids. I've got a little emergency to attend to here." They all hesitated and then began to laugh as they saw what was going on. "Go on the boathouse side of the beach and play with yourselves. Now! You little gutless pricks!" Once, when asked why he spoke in such profane ways to his extended flock, he answered, quite blithely—"cuz I fuckin' feel like it, and they might as well get it from me before some alien huckster takes them to the back shed and prepares them for nothing but the worst."

Bathing his son in the warm lake water of an early summer heat wave, he took off all his clothes, and the boy's, rinsed them, lay them lightly in the sand, and they swam together briefly in the clear shallow water before he sat him near the edge of the beach, submerged enough to hide his child's nudity, and then he ran up to the cottage, buck naked, for the first-aid kit. Wrapping the affronted testicle in off-white bandaging after cleaning the wound and drying it, his wide, muscled arm over the little boy's shoulder was a mixed comfort that would not soon be forgotten.

But that wasn't the story. It was the preamble. As they sat there on the beach, his son grew less and less inconsolable, moving from shriek to sob and then gradually into a much more relaxed state as his dad continued to comfort him. And then, he moved seamlessly from the preamble and started to tell his youngest lad the story.

"Ya gotta take care of those little buggers, buddy. You're gonna need them when ya get older. They'll come in handy, let me tell ya. Ya still got a lot to learn about wiping yer own ass, and I won't always be around to show you how. And those little balls of yours, if you're not careful up there in the outhouse, yer gonna push one right out your own asshole and you'll just end up one nutless little wonder like yer dear old dad. I got one left, though, or you wouldn't be here, would ya? The cancer took the other one; it got all messed up with tumours and shit, and if I'd been a goddamn crayfish instead of a man, maybe it'd grow right back now, wouldn't it? But ya gotta be damn careful with what God almighty leaves ya with at the end of the day. Anything can happen, buddy boy! Hold on to those crystal balls and keep them out of harm's way or they'll fall out your backdoor without so much as a thank you or the time of day. You'll be chuck full of bananafish with no one to help you out!"

Yes, we were thirteen when he told me that story. Our first time, lying there, listening, I wanted him so badly I could taste it. And I think he felt the same way. But the story was enough. He said he knew, always somehow knew it was a tall tale about how his nuts would slide out of his butt if he wasn't careful, but he just couldn't shake the memory of it. And it was an in-joke, the bananafish, between him and his dad and the rest of the well-read world.

That hot summer day, the poppies swaying in the warm breeze as his dad rushed him down to the beach. He had this weird wisdom about it—he always knew, from the get-go, that it was a silly story told by a man with four drinks under his belt before noon, but it was a story he carried in his heart and his crotch for his entire life, from nine when it happened, to thirteen when he first told it to me, and every decade thereafter.

And then, at the end of the first telling of that incredible familial ode, he rolled toward me and we spooned like we always did, and thank the goddesses it was to the left that night or my swollen crotch would have broken that spoon into little pieces and both of our unformed manly little worlds might have fallen out of love with night—or back in. We may never find that out completely.

"My dad, he would always look at me and say one of two things, whenever he got frustrated with my confusion over the simplest ideas. He'd either say, 'Yer ten bricks short of a load' or, 'Let me have a look.' Then he'd stare straight into my clear, green eyes and lightly holler, 'Your eyes aren't brown today! You must be down a quart.' He never just told me I was full of shit. It always had to be a crummy little story. But he loved me. I know that. That's one thing I know for sure."

He told me that story again the last time we spooned. We were both in our early sixties. I wondered if I would ever see him again. It was right after his mother's funeral. She lived close to him, wherever he was, right until the end. His dad had died twenty years earlier. Prostate cancer. Seems the testicle tale had found some silly tragic prophesy somewhere between the balls and mid-rump. We lay there, in the half light, in his little flat in Rome, after the memorial, and then shared copious amounts of red wine in a favoured café. He flew the ashes all the way there and told me there would be a service, very informal, and then a reception in a café, with old friends he knew I'd like to see. He paid all my expenses. I got there, and we were the only ones. He told me later he thought I'd never come if he told me the truth. I would have come. No matter what.

The room he lived in then, in Rome, was sparsely furnished, just a bed, a chair at his writing table by the big window, and a small odd bookshelf, not deep enough for any books, just paper. Everything was white. Especially him. Books were piled on the open plank on the top shelf, and some of them fell on the floor while we slept. We might have finally rolled on top of each other that night, but I cannot for the life of me remember, except for a faint, pleasant sensation in my ass that haunted me for months after. It must have been the wine, or maybe his pinky finally found its way through my crotch and into my heart. Or maybe it was just the story.

But that odd little shelf, stacks of neatly placed paper in between the slim opening, the shelves separated by a single painted brick. I asked him why he didn't have a proper bookshelf. He said, just before I left that morning, still early enough that the light was low and beautiful. He said, 'Count the bricks.' There were ten. He smiled, kissed me, for the first time, on my lips, and said, as he held his own left palm between his legs, lying there, old and haunted, like he was guarding warped, little narratives he never believed but could somehow never let go of.

"I never wanted to be short."

Circles

When I was one I had just begun
When I was two I was nearly new

When I was three I was hardly me
When I was four I was not much more

When I was five I was just alive
But now I am six, I'm as clever as clever;

So I think I'll be six now for ever and ever.
    —A.A. Milne, *Now We Are Six*

As a child, his skin was like a collage of pebbles, small stones. Playing in the sand. Polished and tiny. Hard circles that appeared soft on the outside, rounded and made smooth by their time spent underwater.

New circles rippled among excited splashes above his feet as he sunk into the lake after a perfect dive. At six years old, a perfect dive meant a belly flop, a big splash, and then the light, placid ripples that were left behind. But even at a very tender age, he imagined himself elegant and filled with grace, even when he pranced, then stumbled, in his bare feet on the gravel path leading to the cottage. You could see to the bottom of the sandy lake then: no weeds, no pollution, just clear water and a soft inviting bed. There were huge rock formations rising out of the water at various points. One of them was nicknamed Elephant Rock—on Stoney Lake. Stones and rocks surrounded or covered in water.

He could faintly hear the applause and cheers from his two cousins, his mom, and aunt and uncle, standing on the dock, having finally learned how to swim after a prolonged period of fear and hesitation. They were all so proud, and relieved. It was just over a year since they had finally persuaded him to stop carrying his baby bottle around everywhere he went, empty, just a yellowing plastic nippled prop facilitating what his family was beginning to consider a prolonged oral fixation that was becoming a little embarrassing when company came to visit during summer vacation.

Such a strange, unexpected sight in nature. This lake gamin, this lithe, over objectified, blonde elfin-like creature with speckled pebbly skin, freckled from the summer sun, with perfectly formed legs, like his mother's. He was so tiny, a pale waifish angel wandering around in his childish bathing suit in the baking sun with an empty bottle in his mouth or in his hands. But when he finally decided he was ready to give it up, he filled it with stones from the path to the lake and threw it from the dock. And they all cheered and applauded then too, just like when he finally threw himself into the water after taking so much longer than his cousins to learn to swim without a life preserver.

His dad was up in the cottage, sleeping off a hangover from the day before when he had gone fishing with Uncle Joe. When his dad and Joe went fishing together, they always took a large paper bag and said that it was filled with apples that they would snack on, or sometimes cut into tiny slices with their jackknives to use as bait if the worms weren't working their sacrificial magic. Everyone knew the paper bag was filled with full bottles of beer. He would stand on the dock and wave as his dad and uncle sputtered away in the little aluminum boat with the tiny outboard motor. He loved the look of the rainbow streams of gasoline simultaneously following and fleeing from the churning metal wings, and the way the propeller ripped mercilessly through the water. It felt dangerous and appealing. He was exhilarated and filled with juvenile longing as he felt the sun on his arms and chest and legs, watching his dad steer the arm of the motor and his uncle waving back, smiling.

Years later he met an old grade school English teacher in a downtown Toronto gay bar who just blurted out, in the middle of an otherwise innocuous conversation: "You were just so small, so fragile, and so incredibly beautiful as a child. It was breathtaking to see you in class or walking through the corridors. It wasn't even sexual. Of course, it became that way, as you grew older, into your teens. But as a child, you didn't seem real."

He hadn't remembered this particular teacher. All of the circles of memory seemed to surround each other, as circles do, but they didn't always connect. He always remembered the teacher who wore the robin's egg blue ties and the matching loafers, the one who made a pass at him at eighteen under the guise of paying special attention to a student whose father had just died tragically in a car accident. But that was another short story made long by years of incessant memory having its way with narrative and time.

He sat there, in his teacher's tastefully decorated living room, the fireplace and the hormones raging from one side of the room, not expecting what was about to occur. And when it did, he politely drew away and said, "Your wife is my guidance counsellor."

"Yes, of course. If I wasn't married, things would be different."

Then he politely removed his hand from his young student's crotch and offered him another glass of Coke, thinking to himself, 'It would help if you didn't remind me quite so much of Liberace.'

His mother loved Liberace, but he could never get past the flamboyance, not until he began to recognize his own. Moving from pre-teen angel into effeminate adolescent and then middle-aged queen was not such an easy transition. But he managed with as much grace as he could muster.

At age six, when he came up, breaking through the centre of the faint remnants of the rippled circles left on the surface of the water, after the initial splash allowed the water to regain its composure and move back into relative placidity, the first thing he noticed was his uncle's adoring face, and then his beautiful, tanned brown skin, and then his white bathing suit, and then the circular, slightly elongated curvature of form and fabric, more akin to ovals than circles, that gathered around his crotch and covered what appeared to be a little sack of stones. And then his aunt's slightly bewildered glance.

These circles, they began very early, and blossomed into and out of so many contrasting and conflicted spaces. They looked like circles, separate ones. But when he squinted, they blurred in the sunlight, and like a spiral, they touched.

The Mind and the Heart

On a bitter cold night in Calgary, just before the turn of the last century, I stood waiting for the number one Bowness bus to take me home to my damp basement apartment in a working-class suburb on the edge of an oil rich city. The bus stop was right beside a posh Italian restaurant. As I stood shivering in the cold, a white stretch-limousine pulled up: Tom Selleck got out and went into the restaurant without even saying hello to me. Which was not in the least bit surprising because he had only met me once very briefly when I had worked as an extra in his film, Three Men and a Baby, several years before in Toronto—we didn't actually meet. He just cruised me as he went to his dressing room. I have no proof that he was in fact cruising me, but it makes my life a little easier to bear if I tell myself, once every six to eight months, that I was once cruised by a handsome Hollywood star. He did look straight at me, but that may have been due to the fact that I couldn't stop staring at him. Leonard Nimoy directed the film and spoke to me at one point. He told me to be more animated. I knew he wouldn't have pointed ears, but that didn't stop me from staring at them.

That second time, when Tom and I didn't actually meet, in Calgary, in the winter, I tried not to stare into the restaurant window too often as I waited for the bus. But it just took so long to come, and although I was certain it was Tom Selleck in there, warm and cozy and enjoying fine red wine and pasta or veal or something delicious, I just couldn't stop looking to make sure it was really him. I knew he was in town making a film, so it made sense that the tall, handsome guy who got out of the limousine and looked just like him must be him. But that's the thing about famous people. When I do see them, I can't quite believe that they really exist. Once I shook Pierre Elliot Trudeau's hand in a crowd of people in my hometown, and I wouldn't let it go until I was sure the hand I was clutching belonged to the body of the Prime Minister of Canada. A few more seconds and I might have been arrested.

I have never had sex with a famous person—this late in life, I don't expect to, unless I run into David Hyde Pierce or Nathan Lane or Brent Carver at a fey little bistro one foggy night, and they take pity on me, invite me to their place for some Scotch and intimate foreplay. It strikes me as an incredible improbability that I would probably never recover from. How can one expect to ever fully recover from having had sex with a celebrity? I know I couldn't. It would consume me for the rest of my life. For years, I believed that a close friend had sexual relations with Tony Perkins when he was in Toronto playing the lead in Equus. It turned out that they had just cruised each other in Yorkville one afternoon. But somehow I managed to carry that bit of false information with me for years without realizing it was untrue. I guess I just wanted to believe it so badly. I would look at my friend and just marvel at how he could actually carry on with his life after having had sex with a movie star. I would probably have a t-shirt made and wear it constantly.

My naïve, bordering on idiotic gullibility has never ceased to amaze me. I also believed until I was fifteen that a cousin fell into Niagara Falls on a family trip and survived. It turned out that he fell into the swimming pool at the hotel. Years later, another cousin actually did jump into the Falls. She didn't make it. Needless to say, tragedy and comedy often occur at different times in the same place.

The only thing that haunts me more than the possibility of having sex with a celebrity is the chance that perhaps I did have sex with a famous person once and didn't realize it at the time. Could that have been Mel Gibson or Michel Foucault or John Travolta or Tom Cruise that boozy, giddy night at the bathhouse? With my luck, it was probably Foucault. I am also probably connected to Nureyev in some way, but for the love of God, who isn't?! I did have sex with someone who had sex with someone who had sex with a character on my favourite soap opera. This person, who will remain nameless, took the soap star to his home on a reservation in a coastal Canadian city and his mother was scared the whole time because she thought the guy's character on the soap was such an evil person. I was always very impressed that she let her son have sex with another man in her home. Over the years, the character's moral fibre has improved a great deal. Perhaps it was due in part to his experience on the reservation that night. He had played a young, malicious, restless opportunist. As he grew older and matured, he began to mend his ways.

The soap in question is made in Hollywood, and if you believe in the whole six-degrees-of-separation theory, then I have had sex with every major Hollywood star from the past two to three decades and beyond. Rock Hudson tends to cover a lot of ground in the six-degrees theory since he was a mid-to-late century Hollywood icon who slept around. I must be connected to him in some way, which of course means that I slept, by proxy, and only on film, with Doris Day and most of her immediate family.

But it all just seems so unfair somehow. Once you have fucked the entire Tinseltown A-list, shouldn't that exempt you from ever having to wait for public transit on a bitter, cold night in an oil-rich city while Tom Selleck sits in a warm expensive Italian restaurant, trying to avoid eye contact with the delusional freak at the bus stop who keeps pressing his nose up against the window? I really don't know, and—to use a popular phrase of the day—I'm just saying.

Swish

To those of us who knew the pain
of Valentines that never came
and those whose names were never called
when choosing sides for basketball.
          —Janis Ian, *At Seventeen*

They both hated basketball, but that really wasn't the point, and they never intended to be friends, but that wasn't the point either. There was no point.

"But everything has a point. Even not having a point, that's the point. It's pointless."

That's how it felt anyway. No point to any of it, just an escape from the banal horror of it all. It was more of an alliance, like in a world war, when physical and/or geographic entities so unlike each other in many ways have something to gain from becoming 'friends,' in the loosest sense of the word. And both boys grew up to be very loose men, even though they were only slightly tainted, partially innocent, virginal youngsters when they first formed this awful, allied little duo in the high school gymnasium during the forty-minute period called Physical Education. 'Emotionally Bankrupt Physical Education' would have been a more fitting term for a compulsory activity that divided masculinity and femininity as if they were at war with each other.

There they stood, in their awful navy blue shorts, sweaty

from the run around the football field, and now they were all in the gym waiting to choose sides for the basketball team and then the wrestling team. Swish was a medium-sized teenaged boy with thin, light brown hair and a prematurely receding hairline, and Suzy was a little waifish fairy-boy, eighty-five pounds soaking wet, with a slight lateral lisp and a gait that would have given Cinderella a run for her money at that tragic ball.

"Are you going to the prom?"

"Are you fucking kidding me?"

"Cindy and Donna both asked me. I don't know if I should go."

"Well, the Tonys are on that night, Cindy is fat, and Donna is cross-eyed, but she has nice tits, even though one is a little higher than the other."

"That's not a nice thing to say."

"I wish I had nice tits."

"Cindy and Donna are both really nice girls."

"Cindy and Donna call us names behind our backs and only asked you because no one else will go with them."

"I've never heard that. They call us names?"

"They do it behind our backs, to fit in with the other assholes. They call me Swish and they call you Suzy."

"Suzy's a cute name. Swish is kind of cute too."

"Believe you me, sister, they don't mean it in a 'cute' way."

Swish had a very sophisticated way of speaking. He smoked on the way to school and already had his whole future planned. He was going to become a hairdresser. Suzy's grandmother kept telling him to think about getting a trade, but she never mentioned hairdressing. Suzy had other things in mind though. He wanted to be a writer, or a great actor, or a dancer, or a singer. His father worried that the arts might not be the most lucrative field for him to choose, but Suzy was determined.

Swish had no intention of becoming friends with anyone. He knew his path and stuck to it. But ultimately these two effeminate young men had no real choice. Suzy knew Swish was right about Cindy and Donna, but couldn't quite admit it to himself. While Swish sat alone in the cafeteria eating home-made Caesar salad and exotic sandwiches with eggplant on whole wheat bread and special French mustard that everyone made fun of, Suzy escaped to the library for five full years where Cindy would bring him carrot sticks and olives. Part of the reason he was so skinny as a teenager was because he was afraid to sit alone in the cafeteria and didn't eat lunch for his entire high school career. He always came home after four o'clock with a headache.

He would just sit there in a carrel near the back of the library and read, or just sit and stare at the wooden sides of the cubicle and try not to worry about what any of it meant. There didn't seem to be any point. So his mother gave him lunch money every day, and he would lie to her about what he had eaten and save the money. Family members wondered how he could manage to buy such extravagant birthday gifts and Christmas presents when he had no jobs as a teenager, while all the other boys had paper routes or something they could make extra cash from after school—like siphoning gas from cars in the parking lot at the mall and selling it, or giving the older men blowjobs or being given blowjobs by the same men for five dollars in the back alley behind the bowling lanes. He heard about this from his brother late at night when they lay in their separate beds across from each other in the master bedroom, and his brother would make him tell stories, or wake him to get him a glass of water or—all the way downstairs—lemonade, or make him sing a song to help him fall asleep. His parents were across the short hallway of their small, story-and-a-half, brick-front house, but they never seemed to notice what was going on right under their noses.

Making long stories short was something Suzy and Swish became very good at as they chatted and gossiped for a few frantic minutes, dreading being chosen for a team, hoping they would be overlooked, all the time knowing there would be no avoiding a compulsory high school task where boys were expected to be young men and girls were expected to be young women. There were no alternative arts schools for them in a small-town, nineteen-seventies Ontario environment. But they still did their level best to escape from the inescapable. Ultimately they both did just that in very different ways.

To make a long, predictable story short, Swish became a hairdresser and died in a car accident at thirty-eight, in the middle of a fabulous career as an envied regional stylist who traveled all over Western and Southern Ontario and parts of upstate New York. He was on his way to a convention in Buffalo with his boyfriend. The boyfriend lived to tell the tale, and apparently, it was not a pretty sight. Swish lost his head, just like Jayne Mansfield.

Suzy became a lifelong bachelorette writer and told stories about his life in slightly fictionalized forms, on stage and on the page. Basically he lied about people and himself within the context of highly non-fictional settings and unreliable memory patterns. He couldn't help himself, hard as he tried to be honest. It just seemed like the right thing to do.

Suzy and Swish didn't remain friends after high school, not even for a short time. They didn't really like each other. Swish could sense that Suzy was uncomfortable around him, and it took Suzy well into his twenties to feel the proper amount of shame for being embarrassed by the sight of his own reflection scowling back at him in the mirror. He was Narcissus spitting in the pool, causing ripples to form around the image of something he was terrified of becoming, but already was. Effeminacy shed a very unwelcoming light on young men trying to survive in the fluorescent glare of high school corridors and lockers that kept being vandalized with feces and hateful epithets scrawled in cat blood for no good reason at all by young angry men who were being taught to hate difference.

Of course, there was no cat blood, but at a certain point in memory, one sometimes feels the need to go ballistic in the face of trauma and make it all seem a bit more like a scene from Carrie than a banal, relatively short episode from the lives of two young men nicknamed Swish and Suzy. He felt grateful in a surreal, dysphoric way that his stories had never led to the kind of horrific tales of young men tied to fence posts that he heard about in the news. Sometimes the banal pointlessness of it all was utterly overwhelming—like The Unbearable Lightness of Being. How he wished he had thought of that title before what's-his-name. When he first read the title he thought to himself, "What? The unbearable lightness of being what? The unbearable lightness of being a faggot?"

But there were moments of great liberation—like being a teenaged fairy and suddenly, out of the blue, on the radio, hearing a young American woman sing a hit song about being seventeen in a way that was so unrelated to being queer and yet so disarmingly similar. And then she came out as a lesbian much, much later. Isn't it rich? And then the singer turned queer. Who knew?

Of course, there had been the odd Art or English teacher who tried to sympathize and liberate queer young men from their detractors. But their hands were tied by homophobia, middle-class fear, and a kind of gutlessness rooted in the need for a secure full-time job. Not to mention the hot, muscular, short, stocky judo teacher who repeatedly molested all the straight boys when he got them drunk at the motel after regional judo tournaments. Now there was a whole new meaning for straight that the judo teacher's wife and kids must have had a heck of a time getting their heads around when they all had to suddenly move to Belleville and take the position of superintendent and family in a low-income housing co-op. Years later, Swish and Suzy had a real humdinger of a gossipy bitch-fest one night in a Toronto gay bar where they met by chance. They hissed and belly-laughed about how cute that judo teacher was and how they felt so left out when they learned about the other boys being manhandled by him. They never saw each other again—never really cared to. Brief encounters are often the best kind.

* * *

So remember those who win the game
Lose the love they sought to gain
In debentures of quality and dubious integrity
Their small town eyes will gape at you
In dull surprise when payment due
Exceeds accounts received at seventeen.
—Janis Ian

These are all such long, convoluted stories filled with dubious integrity and the well-slung bitterness of bullied boys moving into manhood. Yes, long stories, and easier to take when they are made shorter and more self-possessed.

Suzy lived a long, happy life, well into his fifties and beyond. He doesn't know how long because it isn't quite over yet. He spends his time balancing past and current trauma through his little, semi-fictionalized tales and trying to see the point to any of it. He became HIV positive in his late forties and found a way, among an incredible community of friends and meaningful strangers, to find a form of well-adjusted joy in the very viral pointlessness of it all. Like the character Michael, who says of his father at the end of the play *The Boys in the Band*, "I never understood any of it," Suzy often finds himself contemplating the utter stupidity of hate. But there is one thing that he has always known about his semi-friendship with Swish: it was essential, and it helped him to learn the truth in so many unreliable and convoluted ways, at seventeen.

Paternity

*Maybe that was the only kind of paternity society could grasp:
the economic.*
> —Edmund White, *The Married Man*

On Sunday evenings, just after dinner, like clockwork, and after a few drinks, he would laugh, call Peter a ballet boy, and then ask him to sing a medley of some of the great songs of the musical theatre from over the past half-century. *So Long Dearie, Summertime, Before the Parade Passes By, You Can't Get a Man with a Gun* were among his favourites. But when Peter would begin the opening lines to something explicit like *I Loves You Porgy* or *My Man*, his father would immediately make him stop. If his father's mood was especially sullen at the time, he would send his youngest son to his room just before *The Ed Sullivan Show* and *Bonanza*, Peter's two favourite hours of the entire week.

When the Beatles appeared on Ed's variety show in 1964, Peter was eight and he knew all the lyrics to *All My Loving, 'Til There Was You, She Loves You, I Saw Her Standing There,* and *I Want to Hold Your Hand.* He lay on the grey carpet in front of the black and white television set and sang them softly to himself, mesmerized by the four prancing images replete with drums, guitars, scandalous hairdos, and very becoming tight, black trousers.

Peter's father, Elliot, could hear the faint childish tremolo bouncing off the screen, harmonizing with these four famous lads, and it pleased him—not only the sound of his son's untrained pitch perfect voice, but the fact that it was delicate enough and soft enough that no one seemed to notice the decidedly feminine sounds coming from the little male body, reclining only inches away from the upright console.

As a voice, it was somehow disembodied, and within the confines of their little storey-and-a-half house on Daleview Crescent, there didn't seem to be any reason to object. And when Peter sang along with Paul McCartney crooning, *'Til There Was You,* an almost ethereal quality passed through Elliot's body, and he thought of the beautiful scene from *The Music Man* when Shirley Jones and Robert Preston sang the very same song to each other. But Elliot always somehow forgot that Mr. Preston just stood there on the bridge while Ms. Jones sang the entire song, and it never occurred to him that Peter was not singing along with four, young, handsome, long-haired British pop stars. He was singing *to* them.

So, when Peter unexpectedly belted out an inappropriate lyric that made it sound like he was, in fact, singing to another man, well, that always set Elliot off and caused quite a stir after an otherwise pleasant family dinner of breaded pork chops, mashed potatoes, broccoli, and creamed corn, followed by chocolate pudding, chilled and poured into a graham-cracker pie crust. Unpleasant words and accusations would fly between Elliot and Jane, Peter's Mom, and the little house would be filled with a troubled atmosphere at least until Wednesday, during which time Jane would take her son aside and ask him to try to remember not to sing those particular love songs when his father asked him to perform for him. Elliot had been craving a miniature version of manly baritones like Harve Presnell, or bass/baritones like Howard Keel, not a tiny, fey replica of Jane Powell, Debbie Reynolds, Doris Day, or even worse, a very young Wayne Newton.

In 1966, when Wayne Newton began to sing Scarlet Ribbons, on episode twenty-eight, season seven of Bonanza, Elliot couldn't believe his ears. Newton's voice was still so young and feminine then, and the repetition of the image of those damn red ribbons in a little girl's hair infuriated Elliot, and when he noticed Peter's high pitched tremolo was in perfect harmony with Wayne's voice, he grabbed his son by the arm and dragged him up the stairs to bed. Peter started to cry, and Elliot swatted him on the side of his neck, exacerbating the injurious pain he had unconsciously inflicted on the boy. Jane wasn't allowed to go upstairs to comfort Peter, and so he slept restlessly all night, on his back, the only way he could get any comfort at all given the severe sprain his father had caused to Peter's left wrist. That was all he needed, a wrist even limper than it had already been deemed.

When Elliot found Jane crying at the kitchen table the next morning, he belligerently asked her what the hell was the matter. When she hesitantly told him about the injury he had inflicted on his son, he looked stunned and walked out the back door without a word. The incident was never mentioned again, but when Elliot took Peter for their usual Sunday afternoon drive along the river road, where he inevitably stopped for twenty minutes to rummage around in the trunk while Peter sat in the front seat, he came back and gave Peter the only hug—and kiss on the cheek—that his young son ever remembered getting from his father. He also whispered, "I am so sorry," but his father's voice was so faint, and so delicate, it didn't seem to Peter that it could be coming from his daddy's throat. And it held the faint smell of rum. Afterwards, they went to the ice cream parlour with very big cones in a little town where the river met a lake. Peter usually only got a small cone.

When Elliot died of a heart attack, he left everything to Peter. Peter was twenty at the time, and his older brother had been estranged since he was a teenager. When they tried to contact him in a small Alberta town, there was no response. In his fifties, Peter would wake up in the middle of the night, after an especially harrowing dream about family, and lie awake for up to an hour trying to remember his brother's name. After slowly going through the letters in the alphabet, a trick his mother taught him as a child, his brother's name would finally come to him—Kevin.

Everyone knew there had been a vicious fight between Kevin and Elliot on Kevin's seventeenth birthday. But no one spoke of it. It was an open secret. Jane had bought Kevin a Janis Ian album as a birthday gift. It was on a list of twelve LPs he wanted. When Elliot heard Kevin and Peter singing *At Seventeen* together in the living room, lying on the carpet beside the stereo he had bought for Kevin the Christmas before, he exploded. Without saying a word, he kicked the stereo across the room, swatted both sons on the side of the head, and sent them to their room. As they lay in each other's arms, in Kevin's bed, across from Peter's matching one, crying, Elliot sat in the living room, stone-faced, with a rum and coke in one hand and a cigarette in the other, thinking to himself, 'This cannot be happening. Not both of my sons. Not both of them!'

Kevin apologized to Peter for not defending him more as a child, told him he was sorry he would have to leave him alone in a few years, and that he hoped they would be together again some day.

As he got older, Kevin often thought of the time he listened to his little brother sing along with Melanie to *Brand New Key* at their grandmother's cottage, and how it was difficult to separate the voices. He would have to go so close to his brother, stand beside him, and listen very carefully, to make out the difference between the two. Elliot had always been a frustrated singer, and often said, while drinking, that his time in the Second World War had given him very little to sing about. Peter followed in his father's footsteps. Frustration was the key element in their family, one they could never fully overcome. But they all knew how to sing about it.

* * *

When Elliot died, Jane's closest friends and family were shocked, insisted she contest the will, and urged her to hire a lawyer and get what was rightfully hers from her husband's estate—but she refused. When the will had been read, only Jane and Peter were present. Peter loved his mother deeply and made it clear to her that he would give her everything she deserved, on one condition. There was a song he wanted desperately to sing at his father's funeral. Jane was, by no stretch of the imagination, a naïve woman. She knew what the lyrics meant. But she also knew that no one else would, and even if there were a few people at the service who had an inkling of what was happening, they would keep quiet about it. And even if they didn't keep quiet, if there were drunken voices at the reception afterwards, the hint of an inappropriate question here and there, well, none of it really mattered, because, primarily, there was a certain satisfaction in knowing that mother and son could send their beloved off with a very special musical message.

The only thing Jane had ever done to displease Peter was when she threatened to cancel their excursion to see *The Sound of Music* at the Paramount Theatre, because he had misbehaved in the schoolyard that morning by trying to join in with some little girls who were playing with their new Barbie dolls. One of the dolls was Barbie as a torch singer, complete with microphone and tight black dress with matching open-toed heels. Peter was so filled with desire he could not contain himself.

He cried when she told him about her plan to cancel the movie, and she quickly realized that the crime did not fit the punishment. She would have to find something less devastating to punish him with. He had been waiting a full year to hear Julie Andrews sing onscreen again, had memorized all of the songs to *Mary Poppins* and sang along in the theatre with his best friend, Laurie. Missing *The Sound of Music* would have had a profound effect on her son's young mind, and by then she knew that she had to do all she could to counter her husband's narrow approach to music and gender.

So, ultimately, the funeral service would perfectly punctuate their mutual attraction to a patriarch whom they loved but never fully understood. And even decades later in middle-age, Peter's tremolo was still intact.

With a large organ behind him, and a thick powerful microphone only an inch from his lips, he filled the church to the rafters.

Once I had a secret love

That lived within the heart of me

All too soon my secret love

Became impatient to be free

So I told a friendly star

The way that dreamers often do

Just how wonderful you are

And why I am so in love with you

Now I shout it from the highest hills

Even told the golden daffodils

At last my heart's an open door

And my secret love's no secret anymore

—Sammy Fain and Paul Webster, *Secret Love*

Ganesh Two

"It's the thought that counts. The gift doesn't matter. Even if it's tacky and you hate it. Don't look a gift horse in the mouth."

He didn't actually mean what he was saying. But he felt he had to say it. In the end, it became a cherished possession. He sat it in his window for an entire summer, and then, in the dead of winter, he began to love him, and it occurred to him that he should be looking west, out the window, and not east and into the room. It didn't seem fair that Ganesh wouldn't have a view. He wasn't like all the other objects cluttering the ledge above his bed. They were just bric-a-brac. This was a god. So he turned him around, and everything changed.

* * *

"What's that smell?"

At first he was offended, tried to ignore his lover's complaint, and just went right on performing fellatio. He said it again, then three more times.

He didn't smell anything, not at first. But as his head slowly rocked, he began to notice a distinct odour in the air, coming from the window. Something was burning.

It all began in the late afternoon. The hot sun was fading on the pale yellow walls. Even in winter, the western exposure gave the room a very warm, summery glow. He had closed the drapes mid-morning. A visitor was the very last thing he had expected, so when the telephone rang twice, two short rings, he just thought it must be the wrong buzzer code and ignored it. But it happened again, and he ignored it again. The third time, he switched on the television to the lobby channel. And there he was.

Ganesh began to simmer. But no one knew except the god himself. For a moment, his eyes played tricks on him. The heat had been building since 11:00 a.m. On the television set (the lobby channel) he could make out a male figure standing by the board with all of the tenants' names on it. So, he walked closer to the screen and immediately knew who it was when he saw the heavy, cable-knit, powder-blue turtleneck. He quickly picked up the phone, pressed the number nine, and let him in. He was short, squat, all arms, with big, round, bicep muscles bulging out, veiny and beautiful in the diminished light. Just as he came, naked on his bed, Lord Ganesh, the little wooden god, burst into flames from the refraction of hot, summer light hitting the nearby crystal ball. It quickly spread to the bed frame, grazed the hair on their legs, then died suddenly with a flicker, leaving a dark trail of black ash, ending in a small damp pool, along the smooth surface of the 1600-thread-count Egyptian cotton sheets he had been given as a gift from a former lover.

"I hated those sheets. They were a birthday surprise. I'm not fond of practical gifts."

"It's the thought that counts."

"Yes. I suppose it is."

And then he looked up, into the window, back at his latest conquest, and whispered, "I love you."

He didn't actually mean what he was saying. But he felt he had to say it. It's the thought that counts.

Ice

I remember the cold night you crapped yourself walking home from your Nana's house, how I always belittled you for calling her Nana instead of Granny, Grandma, or just plain Grandmother. "What's that smell?" I said, as you rushed in the front door and went straight to the bathroom without taking your winter boots off. The odour went through the dining room, into the kitchen, across the living room, and stopped at the fireplace, as though it had made this trip before. This would be difficult for anyone to believe, except perhaps someone already familiar with the depth, substance, and navigational skills of your in-exquisite flatulence.

Our first month together was spent sharing recipes, cooking each other's favourite meals; like chili con carne, or spaghetti and meatballs. Late at night, in the kitchen, you would stay up for hours, preparing for our next gourmet breakfast, while I slept soundly with an increasing waistline and a contented heartbeat.

When you made eggs Benedict for me the first time, I suggested a spinach salad on the side, with real bacon bits, like the brunches I remembered going to in The Village before we moved in together. The day of our first big dinner party, when you had to prepare for seven guests and couldn't find your recipe for stuffed mushroom caps and asked me if I had a good one—you were wide-eyed and frantic in your mother's apron, like an insane chef in some televised cooking competition.

Our friends loved coming to our dinners, prepared especially for them in our little converted carriage house. So many friends visited, and the fireplace made them all want to stay very late and drink in excess and tell stories about their most recent romantic escapades: the accountant who met an ex-astronaut who he took to the Mars café for lunch; the beautician who kept ending relationships with really nice guys whenever she noticed a nose hair dangling from their nostrils; the flight attendant who was afraid the pilot she was flirting with would discover her 'secret' and have 'him' fired; the bellhop who was screwing an enormously wealthy government official from an Arab Emirate and wondered if their relationship would ever amount to anything.

Did our friends think we were interested in their stories because we fed them and listened intently as they slurred their words and spilled red wine on the carpet, costing us our damage deposit when we moved out? Now, I think they probably knew we would never last. We were as hopeless as we had been as children, two boys playing in the same schoolyard, peering at each other through glazed, innocent expressions, wondering what we would be allowed to feel for one another next.

* * *

That night at your Nana's, the ice was so treacherous, and you said we'd have such fun holding each other up the whole way there, but I refused to go. It was like we were totally devoid of metaphor and literally sliding away from each other, but you insisted it would all be okay. Later that night, I tried to drive over to her place to get you but the wheels of my car just spun in the glassy driveway. I fell twice on my way from the car to the back door.

You have such different memories. You recall how beautiful the bridge was as you crossed it alone, like a small girl wearing a red hood in a fairy tale on his way to Grandmother's house, looking for icicles as you peered between the openings in the cement railing, hoping to find a magical one to put in the ice box for her to save for her Christmas tree—and how our love was frozen in time like some eternal chunk of winter glass.

By the fireside, our friends would tell such silly stories about love and romance. One night, giving me instructions on how to love, you told me, "A love will die if you don't treat it like God treats snowflakes, like a fine chef treats every entrée."

I went back to The Village not long ago, after moving to a basement apartment not far from the carriage house that we shared. It was the end of June, and so many of our old friends were there, all dolled up and enjoying the annual festivities. Geoffrey, the one who always brought a dreadful homemade dessert to all our dinners, had just passed away that week. Despite all the stories and the drunken mishaps, Geoffrey had always been there, smiling and ready to help out with those nasty red stains on the pale gold broadloom, hoping, I believe, to stay late enough so I would fall asleep and he could have his way with you, when all he had to do was ask. I sat with Geoffrey's widower, looking across the street at the thousands of revellers, and there were three of our old friends, sitting under the beer tent, laughing and sipping wine from huge plastic glasses, slopping cheap red dollops on wooden picnic tables like they did by the fireplace in our rented home. It started to rain heavily, and he put up his umbrella and locked arms with me, pulling me closer and out of the sudden downpour. When I left him, once the rain had stopped, I walked through the square and glanced at all the names. Three or four stood out—Serge, Victor, Alan—collections of engraved letters identifying some of the people who had passed through our lives. I felt sad, and imagined my own name appearing there. But even if they had been with us that day, we had no place for them to come to dinner.

This is not the way love should unfold. As you told me, love, like food and snowflakes, should be carefully prepared. We only had the beginning; the rest melted away, like fine cheese in the bottom of a fondue pot, or snowflakes on mittens. It's pointless to speculate upon what might have happened. Who expects things to last anymore—did anyone ever? But people do remember our dinners. They amount to something in the minds and memories of a chosen few: the ones we selected from our respective address books, and cordially invited to our home to share one of the many culinary kindnesses we bestowed upon each other daily.

What I remember most is the night you came home with your trousers filled and frozen. The ice. Still, just saying, "the ice," I laugh and my lips kiss yours like magic cylinders stuck to something that attracts them and yet becomes so painful once separated.

No further mention will be made of your 'accident', the way you said "Oops" when you came down the stairs after showering, dangling a laundry bag filled with all your clothing, and how we laughed by the fire, spilled wine, ate homemade pretzels, and made love as you recounted a tale of frozen faeces, and how, that night, when you were on your own, they accompanied you all the way home from Grandmother's house.

My Mother's Purse

"Is that your man-purse?"

"Yes. Are those your man-boobs?"

Someone stole my man-purse the other day. I was sitting on a red, moulded, fibreglass bench in the subway, and I sat Pursey down beside me as I waited for the next train. I never do that, and must have been particularly distracted that day. There was nothing of value in it, just a faux-leopard, portable umbrella, a half-filled bottle of spring water, and some leaky pens. Thank God the umbrella was faux-leopard! Luckily, I had my passport, keys, money, and other important documentation stuck up my ass. I only recall one occasion when someone stole some of my belongings from up there, and it was not an entirely unpleasant encounter.

Within seconds of noticing it was missing, I thought of my mother's purse. I had no desire to run screaming through a crowded subway, trying to find the assailant. Their disappointment must have been far greater than mine.

Whenever something unpleasant happens to me that reminds me of my mother, I always end up thinking it's bad karma to have given her a hard time about superficial things. But like so many people, I misunderstand what karma is, and yet I continue to throw the term around as if I really knew what it meant to pay the piper for all the stupid little things we do in life.

My mother never had anything of value in her purse, and

although it was not fit to eat a meal out of, there were no cockroaches in it. I should have been more sensitive. But it drove me insane. Like me, she had many in her lifetime, but the one I remember most was her last purse. It was one of those mid-sized, cheap, Louis Vuitton knock-offs, and it was presentable on the outside but disgusting on the inside. I would clean it for her every few weeks, but always resented it, and argued with her many times about the state of its interior, and how she should carry it securely over her arm in order to avoid theft, and not like Desdemona's hand-me-down handkerchief about to fall daintily into the hands of unprecedented doom.

My biggest complaint about her purse had nothing to do with hygiene or the way in which she carried it in public places. It was when we were driving somewhere and she would constantly rummage through it, looking for the Holy Grail, I assume, because whenever I asked her what she was searching for, she would look at me with a strained, ethereal expression and say, "Nothing."

Once I shouted, in a very loud stage whisper, "Nothing? You're looking for nothing? Well, 'Nothing will come of Nothing', Mother! Put the goddamned purse away before I drive us into a ditch!" Like some post-modern Cordelia stealing her father's words from his mouth before he has a chance to speak them, I was petulant around my mother far too often.

Once, I was in a play that I had written, and my mother planned to come. Curtain was at eight o'clock, and at eight-fifteen, she still hadn't arrived. She was never late, so I assumed she wasn't coming. We locked the door to the tiny basement performance space and started the show. Not five minutes into the performance there was a very loud banging on the door.

Once she had been let in, she quietly took her seat in the front row, only a few feet away from the wooden lawn chair I was sitting in, delivering a brief monologue about something vulgar, I am sure. Within seconds of taking her seat, she picked her purse up off the floor and began to rifle through it. I could have employed any number of unprofessional strategies. I considered getting up out of my seat, walking over to her mid-monologue, kissing her on the cheek, and gently taking her purse away from her, carrying it securely over my arm for the rest of the performance. I am a cross-dressed performance artist, after all. It would not have been out of keeping with the general mise-en-scène of the overall piece. But I didn't. I ignored her. And I regret that deeply. In life, and on the stage, I have always found improvised, meta-theatrical gestures very comforting.

There was one thing of questionable value that she always carried in her purse. It was a copy of my first published solo performance piece entitled *What Dreadful Things to Say About Someone Who Has Just Paid for my Lunch*. It was dog-eared, falling apart, and filthy. The odd time, she would look at me, and out of the blue, she would say, "How come I never knew about when they hurt you in your book." The first time she asked, I had no idea what she was talking about, so she gently took her fragile copy out of her purse, turned to a page that she had folded at the corner, and explained:

"See, here, where they hurt you."

In the mid-eighties, I was beaten up and robbed in an Athens park by two men who had befriended me and then asked if I'd go to a gay nightclub with them. Over the years, some casual acquaintances (formerly close friends) have suggested that it was foolish to go with them. I do not share their opinion, but I try to respect their right to judge my misfortune so cruelly.

Whenever my mother asked about this incident, I'd carefully explain that I didn't tell her until years later because I thought it would upset her. This odd explanation came from a son who flew into a mini-rage whenever she played in her purse or asked me fifteen times an hour how often we had visited Disney World together. In my most bitter moments, my mother's life strikes me as a terrible distraction that occupied the first forty years of mine. When I am lucid, I know that I was blessed by her bumbling presence, and her frequently conditional love, as she was by mine. I hope she remembers the good times. There were plenty. But there was also a lot of anger and betrayal on both our parts. Perhaps she is in heaven, looking down at me and saying, "You little bitch! It was just my goddamn purse. Leave me alone!" She did swear at me many times, and I swore back. I admired her profanity. Once, sitting in an armchair in the lobby of the retirement home she lived in for the last five years of her life, a man came up to her and said, "That's my chair." My mother, a tiny, grey-haired, sweet-looking woman in her seventies, wearing a pale-orange, calf-length cotton dress I had bought her at the Sally-Ann, which she hated, looked at him and said, "Fuck off."

God bless her.

Once, after a performance in an Ottawa gallery, where I roller-skated with a GI Joe doll sewn into the nether regions of my bright red tights, my mother—after being kept awake during my show by frequent nudges from the curator—walked over to me and said, "Where do you get all your ideas?"

I wanted to laugh and say to her, with light but biting sarcasm, "I am an autobiographical performance artist, mother. For the love of God, where on Earth do you think I get them?" But I opted for kindness and simply said, "From life."

If the subject matter was a little risqué, and it often was, I would sit her down before a show and we would have a little talk where I would tell her that if she had any questions or concerns, she could ask me about them—afterwards. Except for that one general query about where my ideas came from, and the story about my misfortune in Athens, she never did. She was a lifelong fan, and I miss her, fumbling in her purse, driving me insane, and unwittingly foreshadowing all of the things I would become once she was gone.

River & Sea

The river flows both ways.
—Margaret Laurence

I knew there was something wrong when he changed the names of our twin cats from Tabby and Puss to Caspian and Euphrates. They were both sixteen at the time, and I tried to explain to him that they were too old to change and would never be able to learn to respond to such exotic new names. He got angry with me and shouted something about those names not being at all exotic to people who lived in Syria, Iraq, Russia, or Kazakhstan. I don't know how he did it, but he proved me wrong within a day of the sudden movement from classic cat names to the names of a river and a sea. They both began to respond within hours of the change, and as much as it pains me to admit it, they immediately struck me as twin cats who should always have had the names of huge, exotic bodies of water.

The fact that I had told him over a decade and a half ago that a cat can't have a twin didn't deter him from calling them twins when he brought them home from the shelter, so whatever possessed me to think he would reconsider a name change so late in their lives I will never know.

Gosh, was I ever embarrassed, at the tender age of fifty-five, when, only minutes before dumping me, he told me that cats can in fact be twins. I'd just assumed all my life, until that breakup moment, that, because litters were usually more than two, the concept of twins just didn't exist in the cat world. That was so like him, to secretly keep vital information from me, information that might have alleviated my status as an idiot savant just a little—just enough to make me feel a little bit less like some pseudo-intelligent asshole. Silly me. An egg is an egg, and when a single egg produces two offspring, well, that would be twins, whether they're kittens or human babies. Who knew? Apparently, I didn't.

The day he changed their names was the same day he kicked me out. So, understandably, I was in no mood to consider the huge emotional strain of not only losing custody of my beloved kitties, but also having them lose their identities to some misplaced notion of aquatic exoticism—that was too much to bear. So I sat him down and forced him to explain to me—why now? Why, after all these years, did he feel the need to pull the rug out from under all of us, kicking me out and changing their names? It just didn't seem fair, not to mention being sudden, traumatic, and completely uncalled-for. It wasn't like I had cheated on him with someone he didn't know, or, now that we're on the topic, someone he hadn't already cheated on me with. But he didn't know that I knew about that, and I couldn't tell him or he would find out how I found out, and that would just open a whole can of worms that would make me look far worse than I could ever make him look. So, I just accepted his explanation that he needed a complete break due to my infidelity and that he wanted the cats to seem different somehow. I moved out the next morning after terrific breakup sex, and I finally persuaded him after a couple of months to let me have some feline visiting rights. I missed Caspian and Euphrates so much it made me lose ten pounds in a month. I could stand to lose some weight, but I couldn't stand to lose complete contact with those two gorgeous, fucking cats.

He did send me a beautiful card, though. It was a sympathy card and he said he was sorry I was such a prick. But I saw beauty in it, especially the part where he told me that rivers and seas run into each other whether they like it or not, like we did sixteen years ago, like Tabby and Puss did in their mother's womb, surrounded by a bunch of other kittens who weren't even twins, and that he was just feeling worn out by the banal inevitability of life and love.

It rained the day I finally lost it, mid-August, six months to the day after he dumped me. It had been a very humid morning and afternoon, filled with sunshine, turning grey by dusk, when thunderstorms gradually burst through a huge, menacing sky. I just packed up my gear around nine o'clock and set myself up in the backyard, in the midst of a relentless downpour, behind the garage so he wouldn't notice that I was there. I couldn't stand the thought of spending an elegant night filled with beautifully-designed rain and thunder and the sharp explosive cut of lightning sheets so far away from the three creatures I had loved more than anything else in the world. More than Iraq or Kazakhstan or any place where xenophobes think normal names sound strange.

And there he was, standing on his back porch—formerly known as our back porch—calling their new names at the top of his lungs. He was old and radiant in the pouring rain, and if I hadn't seen him through the window a few minutes earlier, pacing the kitchen floor, I never would have known that he was crying. When he came out into the rain, his taupe tank top glistening, his perky little pink nipples erect and drowning, his lovely little swollen tummy protruding, I knew it was the right time. So, I made him cry harder by luring his defamiliarized cats under the cover of my sagging pup tent. And there I sat, with them both purring in my lap as I dried their soaking backs, paying no attention to their own brand new names, and thanking some feline deity from the bottoms of their twin souls for giving them two people who loved them equally and hated each other with such fearless and sudden abandon.

I would wait until morning to return the cats and decide whether or not to take the stolen handgun from my backpack and kill him for being such a callous ex-lover, almost as callous as I had been, but not quite. He should have known better. We were meant to be together, like a river and a sea, whether we liked it or not.

The Shoplifting Nymphomaniac

He knew about the stories of wealthy celebrities who stole from department stores, and when they got caught, came up with elaborate explanations rooted in some kind of implausible excuse: the young actress who was getting into her role as a juvenile delinquent or the ex-beauty queen who claimed she was leaving the store to lock her car—a grey, Lincoln Continental—and had every intention of returning to pay for the merchandise. But he always wondered about the thousands of untold stories about ordinary women who wandered the streets of their hometowns picking up odds and ends for their houses or apartments. He wasn't so much interested in the thievery of men, and was no stranger to this kind of five-finger exercise himself. It was petty crime committed by the opposite sex that he was interested in, because his mother had taught him everything he needed to know about theft, both material and emotional, and he loved her for it.

He remembered the first object he stole from Woolworth's in 1968. He was twelve years old and stuffed a copy of Arthur Haley's paperback novel, *Airport*, into his beach bag on the way home from a swimming lesson at the Lions Pool. Then he boldly went forth into the summer fun section, put a giant un-inflated beach ball into the bag, and quickly left the store. It was thrilling. He understood the appeal. It wasn't the non-existent price that he loved. It was the low-level espionage/criminal aspect that was so enticing.

But then there was the example of his mother. Widowed

and impoverished in her early fifties, she drank what little she had and stole out of need. Standing in the produce section of the local grocery store, her shoplifting defied traditional modes of criminal activity, as she ate bananas and grapes right from the shelves, in full view of store attendants, or took packages of cigarettes from beside the cash register in a small convenience store as the cashier looked away for a few seconds but could easily see what was going on only inches from the till. After being caught for the third time she began to be banned from a variety of shops in her neighbourhood.

* * *

At thirty-two years old, when he looked at his friend Shaylene's puppy, nestled on the old mahogany dresser that once sat by the window in his mother's bedroom, he remembered that he had stolen the satin runner that Marigold was curled up on from a popular imports store only a few weeks before. She had jumped up onto the dresser from the bed early in the evening as he crawled under the sheets with his latest unlikely conquest and began to make love with ferocious abandon. Marigold seemed to be watching at first, growled a little, then quickly fell asleep as the sex developed into a mattress-bending monument to athletic carnal activity. Every so often she would gurgle and sputter, as puppies are apt to do, but for the most part she was an unobtrusive voyeur.

His sexual partnerships were considered unlikely because he was an over-designated homosexual who loved to sleep with women. There was rarely any penile entry—with the exception of one or two occasions when his member got the better of him. But with the passage of time and the gradual loss of instant pulsating erections, he simply took part in what he fondly referred to as male lesbian sex. He once stole a t-shirt that read 'I am a Male Lesbian' at a campus kiosk but never wore it. Very few people took his lesbianism seriously and were dubious about his bisexual tendencies. One friend called his carnal interest in women academic, and all he could think was, 'well, what a lovely way to do research.' Invariably, detractors would ask him whether he preferred men or women. He never knew quite what to say, but the question certainly added further fuel to his erotic performance. He considered all of life a performance and every encounter, sexual or otherwise, a rehearsal for an opening that would never happen. Having been traumatized and emotionally stunted at an early age by intense and inappropriate romantic involvements with a man of a certain age, he was never able to move beyond metaphor and into a world of concrete reality—if it in fact existed in the first place.

His mother's breasts were another matter entirely. He remembered a young woman that he was chumming around with in his teens commenting on how jealous she was of his mother's ability to go braless when she could hardly afford to let her own magnificent, rather cumbersome, breasts, float freely. She had been the first female he had ever had intercourse with. She was a voluptuous, rather heavyset young woman with a crush on him. After working at a summer camp for four months, she returned, for her senior year, a mere shadow of her former self, seduced him instantly, and then fell into a prolonged period of ill-health attributed to radically inappropriate eating habits that allowed her to lose so much weight in such a short time. She gained the weight back shortly after her illness—mononucleosis. She told him that she was baffled by his overtly gay mannerisms when he had been perfectly satisfactory, and surprisingly masculine, in bed with her.

Later in life, he met a large, buxom, English nanny, fell into a confused state of romantic love, and enjoyed a prolonged period of pressing his face into her huge breasts and thrusting his belly and penis against and into her soft beautiful belly and luscious vagina. His confusion was not his own. It surrounded him in the form of startled friends and acquaintances who could not, for the life of them, imagine how this could be happening, and barely concealed their firm belief that he was simply trying to deny his true self. A fey conundrum with a circumcised penis the size of a medium cucumber, he merrily minced through his twenties and thirties as someone who people considered to be as gay as gay can get, despite the fact that he slept with more women than most of the straight men he knew. He had serious boundary issues, hated to say no to people, and slept with just about anyone who asked. And plenty did. Later in life, when people asked why he was so promiscuous, he would just smile and say, "I never knew when to leave the party."

In his sporadic memory and overdeveloped imagination, the subject of his mother's breasts had indirect connections to shoplifting. His earliest memories of them were in the bathtub as a five year old, sitting across from her and being conscious of their small, perfect shape—symmetrical and firm—just hovering above the waterline in the tub. As a much older woman, in her sixties and seventies, they were still quite shapely, and he had vivid images imbedded in his psyche of their consistency and colour—from bathing her weekly. She had grown wan and apathetic in old age and seemed to have lost the ability to enjoy life. She rarely bathed of her own volition, and never shoplifted, smoked, or drank past the age of sixty-nine. Habits had taken their toll on her lungs and bladder and she seemed able to give them up as easily as she had adopted them for over forty years— but not without severe physical repercussions. Emphysema and a weak heart were the price she paid for all that glamour. He would grow middle-aged, without a single regret for paying a heavy price for his own sexual habits.

Once, when his mother stayed the night with him in his tiny apartment, not far from the nursing home she was living in at the time, she stole money from his purse. It was a small satchel that he preferred to think of as a purse. He found the money the next morning stuffed sloppily in the zippered pocket on the side of her handbag. He was angry at first, but his anger quickly subsided when he walked into the room where she was sleeping and saw her, in the morning light, with tears in her eyes. She was sitting on the bed, wearing just a bra and panties, looking out the window at the city. He walked over to her, comforted her, put the money he had taken from her purse in the palm of her hand, and told her she just had to ask—he would give her anything he was able to. Another incident, in his early twenties, a few years after his father had died, occurred when he was in his honours year at University. He was living with her in their family home, and occupying the bedroom he had shared with his brother as a child and through his teenage years. One morning, before dawn, he was wakened by the sound of rustling beside the bed. There she was, on her knees, in her nightgown, bending over his small satchel, taking money from his wallet—her beautiful breasts hanging pendulously in loose cotton, only inches away from him. He took her by surprise by raising his head and whispering, "Mother, what on earth are you doing?" She quickly picked up the copy of Wallace Steven's collection of poetry, *The Palm at the End of the Mind*, that was lying beside his bag, and said, "I was just looking for something to read." Joining the glamorous ranks of wealthy celebrities who had unsuccessfully tried to cover their actions with implausible reasons, her little lie made her a beloved, tarnished star in his eyes. He smiled and told her to just take some money and let him sleep. He had done the same thing as a teenager—wandered into his parents' bedroom while they slept and taken money from the pockets of his father's trousers, but he had never been caught. She was sleeping in the family room during those years, watching Johnny Carson and falling asleep, alone, with the television on. He had memories of his father's sleek muscular chest glistening in the sunlight when he crawled into bed with them on a Sunday morning, in the years before she found comfort in late night TV. They were a desperate lot, his family. Economically challenged and carnally charged, he came by their exaggerated sexuality and their petty theft honestly.

Between the bathtub and the bedroom, he had been primed for a kind of waffling pansexual adulthood that would belie the strong effeminate posture of his corporeal nature. It may have been in his genes, if that were even possible. But one thing he knew for sure: neither one of his parents read the modern poets, but they were both physically beautiful, and they both knew, in their own way, that

> *For all his purple, the purple bird must have*
> *Notes for his comfort that he may repeat*
> *Through the gross tedium of being rare.*
> —Wallace Stevens

tra la

To many men strange fates are given
Beyond remission or recall
But the worst fate of all (tra la)
's to have no fate at all (tra la).
          —Stevie Smith, *From the Greek*

I was so sorry to hear of your stepfather's passing. He was such a lovely man, and I know that he made the past ten years of your mother's life so much less lonely. They seemed like such a pleasant couple, and I saw them together often, from afar, at the mall or the ten-pin bowling lanes, or the zoo and filtration plant where the old engine rooms had been turned into a monkey cage—I always loved the monkey cage, but as I grew older I realized that the monkeys were quite agitated and perhaps didn't like living there.

I once saw them holding hands by the little downtown lake, near the Marina, and then they both stepped into what appeared to be a homemade houseboat with the words *Born Free* emblazoned across the bow. It must have been the one he had built himself.

I always loved that song. It was the theme music used for a film of the same name, and once a friend of mine let her sick, unhappy, little hamster run away into a summer field as she passionately sang

Born free, as free as the wind blows
As free as the grass grows
Born free to follow your heart

I also remember seeing the photo of him in your bedroom at the family home that day when you took me there to show me some of the old dress shirts you wanted to give me. I recognized him immediately and was quite surprised that he even knew your mother.

It always seemed sweet, and funny, that you wanted to give me your old clothes. You have always been so thin, and much taller than me. I still wear some of those shirts. They look quite odd on my short stocky frame, long, but tight, in all the wrong places. I wear the light cotton ones open in summer, with a tank top under them, so it is not as noticeable that the buttons are a little snug when they're closed. Some of the synthetic blends just hang in my closet; I look at them from time to time and think of you.

Your stepfather, I know, was quite annoyed with me for letting you know that I knew him from the past. And I could never quite understand that. But he had his reasons, I am sure, and I cannot expect everyone to live their life as I have lived mine.

I hope your mother is well, and that she still remembers me fondly. I remember her coming to see me as Blanche Bolton in that drag role at the weekly, comic improvised soap. She admired my legs and smooth skin then. Things have changed, but my legs still look pretty good.

What I remember most about your stepfather—and I would never want to hurt your mother by having her know any of this, but I do have a right to my memories, and I believe that I do have the right to share them with someone else that I have loved—I remember his lovely neck. It was thick and red and soft. He told me it happened to men where he worked, something about the automobile plant and all the welding he did, but I didn't understand any of it. I just loved his rough red neck, the tough aging skin, and his full greyish hair. It felt lovely in my palms as I held him there, on top of me, straddling him from below. The weight of a larger man's body on top of my own smaller frame never failed to thrill me.

He told me about his homemade houseboat and how he would take it down the Mississippi every year during his summer vacation. There were times when I felt he was on the verge of inviting me to join him, but he never quite did.

We would meet at the Westbury Hotel at Yonge and Wood. It is now a Garden Marriott and apparently people book months in advance to get suites that overlook Yonge Street during Pride week so they can see the parade from their balconies. I have always loved a balcony. And, of course, I do love a parade.

I am already tired of writing about these memories and have barely started. I am very fickle in my old age and lose interest in even the richest and loveliest things.

I think your stepfather would be in his seventies now. I am approaching sixty, and if memory serves me, which it seldom does, he was at least fifteen years older than me when we first met in the clubhouse that the university allowed our little collective to use for weekly meetings.

First it was GTP, then GLTP, then LGTP. Last time I checked it was LGBTCQO. I always want to call those things GBLT-HOLD-THE-MAYO and sing that old song from the McDonald's commercial—"two all-beef patties, special sauce, lettuce, cheese, pickles, onions on a sesame-seed bun." But I'm sure someone has done that already.

I do not mean to mock political organizations designed to liberate us from strictly tedious sexual conduct, but all those letters just get so confusing. It is not that the good old days were in any way as good or better, but I do think we had less trouble with the alphabet.

Your stepfather took an instant liking to me, which I found very surprising. I was not interested in the least. But he won me over, and we started to meet in Toronto. He would bring rye, ginger ale, and a bag of ice to the room—we would chat, then have sex.

I would like to describe the sex to you in more detail, but I expect that you haven't even read this far, so why bother. I can just think about it, and that will be nice. But if you *have* read this far, then I'll tell you now that, of course, I know why he was upset that I told you I knew him. I had betrayed the closet he had been so comfortable in.

I have always just wanted, in my very unrealistic way, everyone to be just fine with the polyamorous ways of some people. I know that your mother could never get how all of this could have happened. But it would have been nice to have had a friend like her to tell everything to: a friend I could have shared my love of him with. We could have laughed and chatted and had a lovely time. Maybe we could have even talked about the two times that you and I tried to be intimate, but I suppose that would be asking a lot of her.

It was probably good that you backed out at the last minute, just before penetration. I still remember how big it was, and it might have been more than my small arse could handle. But that third time, with your girlfriend—that was lovely, being with both of you—I'm sad, though, that you were drunk and too rambunctious, bullheaded, to just have fun without penetration, since we had forgotten the condoms. But the first part, just lying there with both of you, was so nice and very fulfilling.

I don't think you ever believed me that your girlfriend and I never did anything once you had run off in a huff. We fell asleep for about an hour and then said goodbye. I never saw her again but always remembered her fondly.

She had thick, beautiful thighs, like mine. We both adored your skinny ass. I can conjure an image now, as I write of you, lying between us, long and thin and luxurious, with us at your side, flanking you like voluptuous bookends propping up one slim, hard, satisfying volume.

You told me once that she said, when she first suggested a threesome, that my body reminded her of Baryshnikov's. I was thrilled and flattered, but wondered how she could have imagined such a thing. I never looked quite that good to anyone, including myself.

And you, I thought we would always be friends, and I suppose we are. But like so many people from the past, we remember such strong and passionate bonds—marvel at them, but marvel more at how those bonds have faded, though never in written memory.

Am I just being poetic, sentimental? Of course I am. But I can still imagine kissing you and fumbling in the dark, your thin aging body, your greying temples between my palms—the sensation of your large endowment throbbing between my thighs.

Perhaps you have gained weight and it has grown smaller with age, as some do, and I have no problem with bulk, or shrinkage—as they say, in the midst of that aging pubic jungle, it could very well resemble a button on a fur coat at this late date.

I was wrong when I lamented my boredom before even reaching two pages. I have rambled on and achieved a bit of a tome here, a reminiscence of sorts. I just wanted to say that I was sorry he had died, and that I wish your mother could have had him longer. I had him, and you, for such a very short time. But I have no one to blame for brevity but myself. It was short and very, very sweet. People have often told me that I should not have chosen so many straight men as lovers. But I beg to differ. They chose me. And I feel blessed to have had them all.

There is no opening salutation or closing endearment or a single name mentioned in this memory. Why would I personalize something that is just going to be impersonalized by the very distinct possibility that you will not even read the whole damn thing.

Just know this—here, at the end, whatever it was, between all of us: that to me it was something very thrilling and lovely, and it all crosses my mind from time to time—the lovely shirts, his beautiful red neck, your large lovely penis, her full luscious thighs.

And I hope your mother felt this too, for him. He was a lovely man. She had him for so much longer than I. My only consolation is that I did not want him, or you, or anyone, for any longer than the time it took to laugh and fuck and write and make merry. Tra la.

Suicide Notes...a collection of life-affirming death threats, vignettes, and epithets

> *"you might as well live..."*
> —Dorothy Parker

pansies

She had been knocking on random co-op doors all morning, distraught and looking for someone, anyone, to talk to. When she knocked on his door, he remained asleep in front of his television set with *The Young and the Restless* blaring at 11:00 a.m. He always felt privileged to be able to see a new episode of his favourite soap opera broadcast for the first time every day anywhere in North America from a small Newfoundland television station. He marvelled at all the names of the places mentioned during the brief weather reports interspersed among the commercials—Goobies Bay, L'Anse au Loup, and his favourite, Witless Bay, where he dreamed of retiring. Right in his own country, places he had never heard of and would probably never see. He longed to one day see Peggy's Cove and the Gaspé Peninsula but could never remember precisely where they were. He knew they were somewhere in the East.

He finally got the news just after noon from a friend working in an adjacent co-op. The telephone woke him as he heard the music playing over the final credits of *The Young and the Restless*—made popular as *Nadia's Theme* from the 1976 Olympics, later known simply as the theme from *The Young and The Restless* when Nadia Comaneci's gymnastic excellence had faded into Olympic history and his favourite soap opera began its fourth decade of record-breaking daytime television longevity in the early twenty-first century.

His friend who worked in the neighbouring co-op had called

to make sure it wasn't him who had jumped. He was both comforted and annoyed by her concern.

"Yes, it was me. I'm speaking to you from the spirit world and the long distance charges are out of this world. So fuck off!"

Then he laughed and hung up. But just before he hung up, she said to him—
"Don't look."

But he did. He put his hands on the balcony railing and slowly peered over the edge where he saw her lying in the flowerbed just north of the main entrance to the building. He called the suicide hotline for advice on how to cope later that evening. He wasn't close friends with her, but they would always smile at each other and say hello when they met on the elevator. He told the hotline counsellor about how he remembered one time at a members' meeting when she became a little agitated after making a complaint that everyone should not have to pay for satellite television because she didn't even have a TV. One of the board members hastily explained that it was a vote, and became a little haughty when he told her, in a perhaps unintentionally condescending manner, that this was how a co-op worked, and if she wanted change then she should come to more meetings and make her feelings known.

Her feelings were very apparent after she leapt, and there was a tasteful sign in the lobby a few days later with all the information about her memorial at a nearby chapel. He wanted to take her a bouquet of pansies, tied with a ribbon and a light blue paper doily wrapped around the stems. But when he looked at the sign and noticed that right beside it there was another notice regarding the next meeting of the gardening committee, he felt a little disgusted and decided not to go to the memorial. It seemed obvious to him that they were meeting, so soon after her tragic incident, to discuss repairs to the flowerbed.

He would just steal a small bouquet from the roof garden,

light a candle beside them, and put them in his apartment window overlooking the garden she had so unceremoniously landed in—flattening the petunias, disturbing the soil, and splaying the peonies into one oversized, ruined corsage.

crossing

He hadn't been back in well over a year, ever since she had made her shocking decision. As they walked through the grounds of the State Park, they chatted about this mammoth, iconic division between the two countries.

"Even as a child, I never felt that way. Everyone kept saying our side was better, that we had a better view, but then we'd come over here, away from all the over-manicured flower beds and the tourist-trap hotels, and much later the casino and the weird midway with the haunted museums and the wax figures of mostly-dead celebrities. Fuck. This side is way more laid-back. It kind of blows the whole myth out of the water that they're not as friendly and way more commercial than we are."

His companion that day, at the State Park, didn't say much as they strolled toward the little bridge that led to the majestic, terrifying precipice, overlooking the narrowest portion of the Falls. He just smoked and laughed along at the odd, tasteless joke being made at the expense of the young, the restless, the suicidal, and the dead.

"My life is so tragic, 911 calls me."

He had somehow forgotten, when he first invited his friend to come along, that his friend had once tried to take his own life by wrapping his head in electrical tape and then panicking at the last minute, successfully ripping it away from his mouth just before the early tremors of asphyxiation took effect. He might have reconsidered taking him with him on this dark pilgrimage if he had remembered in time.

As they stood at the edge of the Bridal Falls, the water gushed over the rocks like its namesake—a thick gauzy swatch of translucent matter cascading like a procession of beaded, layered whiteness into a fateful union with all that it met and married at the bottom of this interminable ritual of life and its inevitable ending.

He muttered something to his friend as his friend smoked, leaning against the strong, stone wall along the edge of the escarpment. He didn't hear him, but he laughed anyway.

"Mortality. I've learned to live with it."

They took photos, went for lunch at the Red Carpet Inn across from the gates to the State Park, and bought souvenirs at a gift shop. As they drove back across the Rainbow Bridge, he remembered his smoking companion's brief brush with suicide and tried to apologize for being insensitive by asking him to join him on his first visit to the site after her shocking plan had played itself out.

His friend smiled, puffing all the way across the bridge, even though it was a rented car and they would probably get fined for the smell of smoke inside. The rental agency had been very clear about this. He took a drag on his cigarette, blew it directly toward the driver, as the awkward apology was being made, and smiled, saying,

"It's okay. It was nice to get out for the day, to be with you, enjoy the beautiful weather, and, you know, I'm sorry about your cousin, but at least she succeeded. I don't even know why I tried. And I failed, again. And fuck, that duct tape hurt like hell coming off."

"I thought it was electrical tape?"

"No. It was duct."

"What colour? Fuck, I always thought it was electrical tape cuz it always made me think of that wild, Richard Gere gerbil myth."

"I never believed that. Red. The duct tape was bright red."

"Cool, red. Bright red. Thank you for coming with me today. It helped a lot to see the Falls again, for the first time, after she died there."

It was late in the afternoon, and as they approached the border, ready to brave anything customs officials might have in store for them, they smiled at each other and found a little comfort in the security of their mutual, half-hearted remorse.

This was an easy crossing. The man in the booth just asked for their passports, how long they had been there, their citizenship, why they went, and if they had bought anything.

"Six hours."

"Canadian."

"To see the Bridal Falls."

"A couple of postcards and a souvenir ashtray for honeymooners."

postie

According to his online research, women were less likely to jump into the Falls. It was one of the seven wonders of the world and had somehow been reserved for mostly men when their final leap sprang to mind.

Some actually survived. Others did it in a barrel as an elaborate stunt. But his cousin didn't. She had planned it all very well and apparently looked quite serene as she floated toward the edge, her head above water for the very last time. He was ten years younger than her; he'd admired her cover-girl beauty as a child and often emulated her in his feminine imagination. She had been a math teacher, was loved by her students, always had a big bowl of Jolly Ranchers on her desk to share, and probably knew a lot more than he did about odds, statistics, and all that. But he knew about gender and how sad and unpredictable it could be if it was ignored, repressed, left unattended...

He got the news from another cousin who told him that the victim's sister—his estranged cousin—found some comfort in the knowledge that the photos taken of her sister as she was swept along the last short stretch before the edge of the Horseshoe Falls, on the Canadian side, revealed a very peaceful look on her face.

His research also uncovered the disturbing yet practical tendency of horrified onlookers, often tourists, to take snapshots and then deliver them to a local police station in the event that the body was never found, or worse perhaps, if it was not identifiable upon discovery. Hers was able to be identified only by her teeth and wedding ring. So, the knowledge and ensuing comfort of the photo became, for her sister, a saving grace.

Several years before her suicide, he was singing one night at an open mic in a local queer cabaret and had heard that afternoon, from a friend who worked in the office of the co-op adjacent to the one he lived in, that one of the members in his co-op had taken his own life by jumping from the Niagara Escarpment. The Falls were just a few miles down the road along a tree-lined scenic route. His body was never found, but they did find his car, and there were eyewitness reports that a short man in a postal worker's uniform was seen walking along the edge of the Escarpment during the late afternoon. When the police opened the trunk of the car, there were piles of undelivered fashion magazines that, according to the postmarks, had been there for several months.

At the cabaret, before he sang, he explained to a small, inattentive audience that he had been given the sad news about an acquaintance who lived in his building earlier that day, and he wanted to honour him by singing a song he had written years before about one of his favourite destinations. Someone he didn't know, sitting at a small table near the stage, spoke up and said— "I knew him. He was my friend."

One of the verses of the song was: "Some folk jump into Niagara Falls, and although it's sad, I can't recall, a more sensational suicide, a classier way to decide to die, at Niagara Falls, Niagara Falls..."

The audience member didn't seem disturbed by the lyric and applauded lightly after the song ended.

As he walked home from the cabaret that night, he remembered the first time he had met him—on the day they were both picking out their units a month before the co-op would open. He noticed how short he was, about five-foot-five, with a beautiful face, a tanned fit body, and a disarming smile so bright and sincere it could make a stranger blush. They chatted a little and he said—"I'm a postie. I deliver mail in Rosedale to rich people." And then he chatted on about how excited he was to be moving into a co-op in the gay area of town and that he hoped to join a bowling team, a bridge club and possibly the gay men's choir, if they'd have him.

Just like his cousin, the postie ended up driving a considerable distance toward a final destination. She made her way across the Peace Bridge to Fort Erie, then along the Ontario scenic route where he had written his song about the Falls many years earlier on his way to visit his American cousins. The postie had driven from the largest city in Canada and then along another scenic route connecting a small tourist town to one of the seven wonders of the world—dramatically dividing an eastern portion of two of the world's largest countries.

A few months later, he heard that the postman had been diagnosed with HIV and had become very depressed. Not long after he leapt, anti-retroviral medication became much more effective, and people in countries with reasonable health care lived happy lives for decades—talking on the telephone, watching their favourite soap operas on satellite TV, singing songs about natural wonders, playing cards, bowling, reading fashion magazines, and worrying about the future...

"Sad lives, filled with secrets, but happy."

Niagara Falls *(to be sung)*

I've lived my life in scenic spots from the Rockies to Gaspé
I've seen the Northern Lights both on and off
I've swam in Hudson's Bay
I've entertained in igloos from the Yukon to the Pole
I sprayed graffiti on the Great Wall
I saw through the black hole
I was bored by Xanadu

I've seen Mount Rushmore
more times than I care to recall
But it's not a lost horizon after all

Slowly I turn, step by step
my throat dries up and I lose my breath
at Niagara Falls, Niagara Falls

Where they call me The Maid of the Mist
cuz that's where I got my first wet kiss
at Niagara Falls, Niagara Falls

I don't expect to ever wed
but long before i'm good and dead
I'm gonna spend someone's honeymoon
in a cheap hotel in a sleazy room
at Niagara Falls, Niagara Falls

Well some folk jump into Niagara Falls
and although it's sad I can't recall
a more sensational suicide
a classier way to decide to die
at Niagara Falls, Niagara Falls

A wonderful place for you to be
Marineland and Game Farm
Niagara Falls, Niagara Falls
Niagara Falls, Niagara Falls

showdog

The gentle caresses of his hand thrust deeply into her vagina. The passionate kissing. The tenderness of her soft, round belly and her small, firm, peach-like breasts against his chest. Years later, he couldn't remember if there had been penetration, but when he saw her, over two decades after the incident, they drank heavily at dinner, ate thickly breaded pork chops, laughed with his cousins as they all reminisced about the past, and at one point, she said, "You were the best lover I ever had."

They were all quiet for a moment. No one knew what to say, but didn't seem at all bothered by the remark. It was flattering, though he didn't really believe her. And yet it didn't matter whether it was true. If she believed it long enough to say it at dinner that night, then that was good enough for him. He just touched her hand, smiled, and took another bite of his breaded pork chop. It was delicious. The best he had ever had.

When they told him she was in hospital, ten years before he saw her again, and that her son and many of her friends were very angry at her for what she had tried to do, he remembered how, that night so long ago, she had ended up in his room in the first place.

She was his cousin's best friend. They were both staying overnight at the cousin's house. The next morning she explained to him that the edge of the thick, shag carpet in the renovated basement had been raised by the cousin's prize-winning Doberman's unclipped toenails, and when she went downstairs to go to bed, the half light in the hallway concealed what was blocking the door to the bedroom. She thought it was locked. So she walked across the narrow hallway to his room, knocked lightly on the door, let herself in, and crawled into his bed.

He always found the memory of her explanation so flattering, and thought that the Doberman had been a lucky talisman for their brief sexual encounter and lifelong connection. However, he felt such sadness that her family couldn't see her suicide attempt some other way: that she was just very sad, and it seemed like the only answer at the time. Why couldn't they just be grateful that she hadn't succeeded? Wasn't failure, in fact, the greatest triumph for the failed victim's loved ones? But maybe they were right and he was wrong. He did always have a way of mistaking peoples' love for someone as misdirected and much too invested in the serious everyday workings of the human psyche. Love and life just needed to be fun and fleeting. The sad parts had to be accepted with dignity and grace.

But despite his forgetfulness regarding actual coitus, he did remember very clearly how lovely that night had been, and how beautiful she had appeared to him, so suddenly, after the Doberman's unclipped toenails directed her toward his room in a very unexpected way. She lived for such a long time after that and never once did she fail to mention, when they had the chance to meet again, how much she had enjoyed that one-night-stand. And he wondered, all through the years, how someone who professed to be gay could have become her favourite lover, and how she could have lived to become his as well.

convertible

Whenever he heard her say it, he would take a deep breath and whisper, in a soft kind voice just loud enough for her to hear, "I love you, and I hope you never do that. It would be very sad for everyone who loves you."

She somehow knew enough not to push him any further, because the deep breath that he always took whenever she said it gave him away. Even though the words that followed the breath were kind, and spoken in a loving way, she could tell just how angry he really was.

It was a very hot summer day when she said it for the last time. They were walking along Aylmer Street—a convertible drove by and the driver honked the horn and called out to them. Just a wave, a simple hello and a smile. It was someone they both knew and wished they could have spent the day with instead of each other.

As they continued walking, they eventually left the sidewalk and took a diagonal route along a stone path and through a small park surrounded by a half dozen, huge, perfectly formed evergreen trees. The small park was on a corner lot where the Salvation Army Temple had been for years. An older section of the building had been demolished more than a decade before, leaving room for the park and the trees. There was a single bench and a small bed of flowers. She said it—the usual utterance—just as they were passing the bench.

"I'm so stupid I wouldn't even know what to do if I had the nerve to do it."

He took the customary deep breath and began to move his lips, but the heat, and the memory of the honking horn of the convertible had made him more irritable than he might have ordinarily been. He whispered. But there was nothing soft or kind about it this time.

"I can tell you how. There are many ways to do it. You could slit your wrists or drink Javex or jump from your tenth floor balcony or overdose on Valium, or…" And then he stopped, half-ashamed and angry with himself for giving in to what he had suppressed for such a long time.

She didn't respond to his momentary outburst, and she gave him no reason to think that it had bothered her. She knew how far she could go with certain subjects. And on that day, in the small park, after wanting so badly to be with other people in a convertible, and not with him, with the summer air hitting her face and blowing through her greying hair, she unwittingly discovered that this would be the last time she could raise this particular issue with such unwitting nonchalance.

Having brought him into this world, she loved him deeply— enough so that he was the only one she could say this to, and being away from him, anywhere, without him, in a car, with mutual friends, with the top down, seemed like an appropriate place to forget why she even felt this way in the first place. So when the car horn blared and their friend smiled and waved as he drove past them, she might have felt that this would be the right time to say it again. But she was wrong. It would be the last time she would ever say it to him. He wouldn't have it any other way.

flocking

At first they thought she was brain-dead, but she fully recovered and lived quite happily for several years afterwards. She had been at a play the night before, a dramatized version of the short story *The Yellow Wallpaper*. She blamed her daughter for the attempt. She didn't want her only child prancing around the stage in fancy underwear pretending to be a madwoman who could see human forms moving in the patterns on the walls. She just needed rest and relaxation. Her daughter's activism and artsy activities served only to make her more jittery and discontented with her life.

She had just taken her final bow after the third curtain call when she noticed the stage manager looking very distressed in the wings. When she got to the dressing room, the whole cast of five women were already there, still in their white period underwear, from the Victorian era. The stage manager walked in after her, and they all sat down together to give her the news.

She had heard it so many times before that she just laughed, poured herself a shot of scotch, neat, and said—"My mother is not brain-dead. She'll be fine. She always is. This is her way of being dramatic. I have mine and she has hers. She just does it off-stage, and I do it on."

She would be in a coma for six days, but somehow the stage manager had misinterpreted the news from a very distraught relative and managed to relay the message with the word *brain-dead* in it. It had been pure speculation on the relative's part, but it sounded very concrete when it was told to the stage manager on the telephone just after intermission. By then, it was too late to stop the second act from proceeding.

They did the show for the next six nights, and for the entire time, the brain-dead diagnosis lingered in the minds of the whole cast and crew. The closing night party was very sombre for the first few hours, but after a lot of drinking and repressed sadness, everyone just let loose and danced and laughed well into the wee hours of the night.

The large, green room (which wasn't green at all except for a couple of overstuffed cushions and a fake palm tree), where the closing party was held, had heavy burgundy wallpaper on one wall behind the overstuffed chesterfield that had been used in a production of *The Importance of Being Earnest* a few months before. Just before the call came from the relative who was camping out in the waiting room at ICU (the same relative who said *brain-dead* at least three times during the initial call), she was lying on the couch laughing and suppressing tears about her mother's state of unconsciousness, and said, between tears and chuckles, to one of the actresses who was still wearing her period underwear—"This wallpaper is made of velvet. I love it. I can see your vagina in it."

"Flocked. It's flocked."

"What?"

"The wallpaper. It's not velvet. It's flocked. It's called flocking."

"Well then, flock you sexy."

They rolled around on the couch making out and laughing when the stage manager entered the room and broke the good news. It put a damper on the last hour of the party. They had all been so happy due to the abandon they allowed themselves to feel once a few drinks had set in, and she had been so insistent, all through the rest of the run, that her mother would survive. But somehow the news of her mother's imminent recovery put them all back into a deep awareness of how sad the attempt had been.

The cast and crew lingered for another hour, gave the customary closing night hugs to everyone, including the people they hated, and went home. She stayed with the costumed cast member—they disrobed and made love on the couch. As she was falling asleep, imagining her random lover's vagina quivering in the deep, red patterns of the flocked wallpaper, she thought of Oscars Wilde's final words in the hotel room in Paris where he lay dying, after a lifetime of wild success and extreme oppression.

"Either this wallpaper goes or I do."
Oscar didn't survive the wallpaper. Her mother did.

transit

They were on their way to a post-modern production of a famous psychological thriller when his companion said to him:

"Can we take a cab? I'm afraid of the subway today."

"Sorry, I budgeted for tokens this month. I can't afford to split a cab."

He didn't offer to pay for the full cabfare and didn't seem bothered by the refusal to entertain the possibility of an alternate mode of transit; nothing more was said about it as they entered the subway station.

Standing in the designated waiting area (DWA) on the platform, his friend took him by the arm and said,

"Let's sit on the bench while we wait."

They sat in silence until the sign read one minute before the train would arrive. His friend then exclaimed, in a timid, slightly manic way,

"Some day, I might have to just walk over there and step in."

He looked at his distraught friend, put his hand on his shoulder, wondering whether the play would be any good, and remarked, with as much thinly concealed annoyance and reserved compassion as he could muster:

"Well, I guess it's up to me then."

As they got up to walk into the subway car, his friend looked at him and said,

"What's up to you?"

"It's up to me to remember to never travel on the subway with you again."

The play was very well done, with a lot of beautiful young men moving acrobatically across the stage as they played at being psychotic. They took the subway home together and agreed that it had been a perfectly lovely evening out at the theatre.

seventeen

In 1973, naïve and very young for his age, he sat on the edge of his parents' bed with a cheap bottle of red wine, thinking that if he drank it all in less than five minutes, he would die instantly. He was wrong.

In 2016, at the age of 59, he sat in his living room with five unexpected bottles of the best Italian wine under ten dollars—according to a national newspaper—in an LCBO carrier bag under the kitchen table, and wondered how many years of his life he would lose from drinking. The unexpected bottles were the result of a miscalculation regarding the number of seasonal parties he would attend during the last ten days of the final month of 2015.

A quick tally in his head, based on nothing scientific, or even reliable, got him nowhere fast regarding the effects of elderly grapes on a compromised immune system. He never expected to live past fifty, forty, thirty, twenty. He had been relatively care-free until he was ten.

Generally speaking, the odds just did not seem to be in his favour when it came to longevity. But he had been wrong all along. He disagreed when people uttered that old cliché in his presence— "Life is short." He felt he had enjoyed a long life, much longer than so many he had known who had died very young.

Six decades of expecting mortality to quickly take its toll had been a reasonable way of wading through all that came his way. He had heeded Chekhov's warning from his undergraduate years— and he had taken it to heart—about "a sad life, full of secrets, but happy." He knew he had the quotation wrong, but this was the way he liked to remember it. And the other line from Chekhov that he treasured was: "I am in mourning for my life." It gave him great comfort, mourning did. Light, constant mourning, pitched with a pale melancholy glow. It seemed like a perfectly reasonable way to prepare one's self for the inevitable results of being mortal.

But taking his own life, halfway through his teens, as he perched on the edge of his parents' bed—young, bold, naturally blonde, and relatively free—entertaining the very unrealistic possibility of death by cheap wine: that was his one and only attempt at suicide.

Ultimately, mortality occurred to him as the only viable option for someone like him. It was just something that seemed to make sense, not long after that very formative failure at seventeen...

carrel

He didn't know him very well. They never spoke, not that he could remember. But he did know his girlfriend. She was always in the library during lunch period, and she would come over to his carrel to chat for a few minutes. He would hide the carrot sticks, celery, and the three small pieces of cheese, wrapped in wax paper, in his large pencil case. He spent all his lunch periods in the library. Being too shy to sit alone in the cafeteria, he felt it was his only option.

The day it happened, she didn't appear beside his carrel, and it gave him time to enjoy the carrots, celery, and cheese without having to quickly hide them before she came to chat. Food was not allowed in the library. They usually just talked about upcoming quizzes and exams, books they were reading, and sometimes she would hint at what boys she thought were cute, even though she knew this made him uncomfortable and strangely curious.

He didn't get the news until the last period of the day when his American History teacher walked into the classroom wearing his customary, colourful tie with matching loafers. On this particular day, the shoes were a peculiar shade of pale blue and the tie was paisley with touches of the same blue evenly distributed through-out the pattern. He loved paisley all through high school but was afraid to wear anything that would draw more attention to himself.

Just the week before, she had come to his carrel a little upset about the prospect of not having a date for the upcoming prom. He timidly asked her if she was still going out with the student council president. She laughed a girlish, high-pitched laugh, much like his own, but he would never laugh that loud in the library, or anywhere in the school. And then she said—"I don't know. He's being difficult. He says he doesn't think he wants to go with me, or anyone."

But he was the president. Didn't he have to at least make an appearance? He was gangly, pock-marked, very mild-mannered, and extremely well-spoken, and his girlfriend was not considered much of a catch among the jocks and the popular young women who dated them. They always made fun of them as a couple but probably voted for him for president because he was very smart and always did the right thing in the interest of all of the students. In the fall, he had lobbied for extra funding for the football team, which seemed odd because he never went to any games.

So, when he heard the news in American History class, he was shocked, like everyone else. And the way the teacher told it made it seem even more shocking, and unnecessarily demeaning to the rest of the student body.

"I have some terrible news for all of you. Our student council president has taken his own life. He shot himself in the head with a hunting rifle and was found in his parents' garage early this morning. He was a wonderful, intelligent young man, and he was a sensitive and caring person who shone so much brighter than so many of you. Please go home now. I'm dismissing all of you early. This is shattering news. I'm shattered, and all of you should be too." And then he turned on his pale blue heel and left the room.

As he walked home from school that day, he remembered the time when the dead student council president, after making a beautiful speech about postsecondary studies abroad, walked down the three steps from the stage in the school auditorium and tripped on the second step. He fell headlong into a podium stored beside the stage and had quite the bruise on his forehead for a couple of weeks. There was complete silence. He just picked himself up, looked very flushed and embarrassed, and then took his seat beside his girlfriend in the front row as the school band began to play *Oh Canada* followed by *God Save the Queen*.

He could tell that some of the students assembled that day were concealing their laughter when this mishap occurred, but the president was so respected and revered for his work with intramural athletics, well-funded field trips to historic aboriginal sites, improvements to the bleachers in the football field, judo tournaments, bold library acquisitions, the Kiwanis Music Society, the annual Gilbert and Sullivan revue directed and designed by the American History teacher, the drama club, and new innovations for young men interested in Home Economics, that no one dared laugh when he fell. He had been way ahead of his time, and it was tragic that his time had passed so quickly.

As he walked by the house where the president had lived, he could see the closed door of the garage, and he wondered whether the president's 'widowed' girlfriend was still annoyed with his indecision about taking her to the prom, or whether to go at all.

rifle

It was a tiny room with just enough space for a vanity and a small bench where she could sit in front of the mirror and apply makeup, or gently rummage through the little drawers on either side for nylon stockings or the red half-slip she wore under skirts for special occasions: the slip her youngest son would try on when no one else was in the house, holding it under his arms so it looked like he was wearing a knee-length strapless frock.

Until he was seventeen, his parent's bedroom was a little haven he could use when the house was empty, playing at the role his mother had become so discontented with. After returning from the second-world war, marrying a beautiful twin in the late forties, and having two sons by the middle of the nineteen-fifties, his father's drinking took the place of the love that had begun so suddenly after the war, then ended as suddenly when marriage and unexpected poverty plunged them both into forms of sad suburban depression and class humiliation.

Struggling at the edge of the bed with his father, his mother at his side assisting with the struggle, was such a faded shocking memory to behold whenever it returned. The rifle had been one of his dad's hunting rifles, usually stored in the basement on a gun rack his brother had made in woodworking class in high school.

They heard his father crying and knew he had been drinking heavily all morning. When they got to the bedroom, there he was, sitting on the edge of the bed with an empty mickey bottle of rye on the end table and one of the rifles in his lap, like a guitar stretched across him as he cried and sang *Red River Valley* to himself, gently strumming the edge of the gun metal as though it were a musical instrument. His mother spoke first, angrily:

"What in the hell are you doing with that thing up here?"

It was obvious what he was doing, or about to do. They both walked over to him, took an end of the rifle, and pulled it gently away from him. Although it was perceived as a struggle, and remembered as a struggle, he put up very little resistance as his wife and youngest son took the weapon away from him. And then his mother slammed the bedroom door and shouted—"Sober up."

She put her arm on her son's shoulder as they walked down the stairs to the first floor of the small storey-and-a-half house they lived in. As she walked toward the basement door to put the rifle back in the handmade gun rack she looked at him and said, "There aren't even any bullets in the goddamn thing. He has no bullets. Hasn't used those guns in years. The damn fool!"

But somehow, whenever he remembered that struggle with his father and the rifle, the idea of bullets was never very far from his mind—and how he had looked at her as she took the rifle back to the rack, when he said, quietly and lovingly,

"Mother. Please be quiet."

virginia

> Gone, dreams of the past,
> Gone, with a love that moved too fast.
> Gone, bright shiny days,
> Gone, in a young and restless haze.
>   —theme song from *The Young and The Restless*

Their bodies would swing and flow like taut, sinewy, identical hammocks of muscle-bound skin and bone. He wanted to lie among them, befriend them, do what boys his age did then in the privacy of their own homosocial bonds. But all he was able to do was catch a glimpse of them in the high school gymnasium as they mastered the pommel horse and the rings and the floor exercises and the far-flung wild beauty of the trampoline. Only a couple of years later, the floor exercises would make an iconic connection to the theme song for a soap opera that he began to watch as a teenager and continued into his sixtieth year. But they were long gone then, those beautiful twins who competed in gymnastics.

He had his own talent for the pommel horse, but the gym teacher seemed aloof around him and hesitated to give him the guidance he needed to craft his small feminine frame into a regimented, finely tuned instrument for precise athletic display. His gym teacher wouldn't dare offer supporting gestures with a feminine male body—not like he would with the masculine twins—spotting them by holding his palms gently under the front of his prized students' identically muscled torsos, as he assisted them with the rhythms and bodily movements of their chosen sport. But despite the restrictions placed on the teacher's manly gaze, he humbly tried his hand at it all, displaying a youthful knack that was never attended to. So when he flew from the springboard that day, luckily sustaining no injuries as he gracelessly landed between the board and the pommel horse instead of flying swiftly over it with his arms placed firmly on the hard firm surface of the apparatus, he knew that this would be the end of the line for him—his last hope for excellence in gym class dashed like a sentence turning backwards upon itself and landing in the middle of a poorly constructed metaphor.

The twins went on to win acclaim in national competitions and then enrolled in a military college right out of high school. They both excelled, and continued into families and marriages that appeared, from a distance, to be the perfect, identical outcome for their perfect, identical lives. They looked so much alike when he saw them leave their house for high school every morning, only a few doors down from where he lived. He admired the easy camaraderie and boyish physical affection they shared— if there was any uneasiness within the competitive nature of the athletic fields they pursued, it was not visible in their brotherly bond. They appeared to be having interchangeable lives. The fact that they both achieved excellence in all the same things, both scholastic and sporting, contributed to this seemingly well-balanced, lifelong exchange.

When he got the news that one of them had shot himself while living on an American military base in Virginia, it was shocking to consider the position of the remaining twin. Over the years, he could never quite remember which one had died so tragically. Decades had passed since high school, and *Nadia's Theme*, as a gymnast's anthem, was a distant memory. But its incarnation as the theme song for a long-running daytime melodrama still lingered, late in life, within his daily routine. He would often watch it at 11:00 a.m. as he began his late morning ritual of emails, editing, and making sure his medications were all arranged and in order by the bathroom sink. At 11:00, when he swallowed his first tablets, the first few notes of the iconic music would rise up from the other room as the hour-long soap began. He would tune in and out of watching sections of it as he checked his email, Facebook, and text messages. If he was tired from late-night editing and writing new reminiscences, he would sometimes just lie on the couch and attentively watch the entire episode, or drift off to sleep sporadically as the drama unfolded. Some of his friends and colleagues thought it a trivial obsession. But he considered it a strong, warm connection to a televised family of forty years that he could bond with and then switch off once the trauma, the divided love, the confrontation, the strained familial warmth and implausible story-line ended at noon. An affordable satellite television package in the co-op where he lived much of his adult life made it possible to watch it four or five times a day if he chose to, all from different North American television broadcasters. Usually he watched the earliest telecast direct from Newfoundland, a part of his own country he had never visited after four decades of travelling to so many other places. He would only watch it again if he had slept and missed a pivotal section of social dysfunction or romantic mayhem.

He had been to Virginia once, on a road trip to visit a friend's sister. Years later, he became acquainted with the acronym 'a **H**ouse **I**n **V**irginia' as a way of referring to being HIV positive:

"He has a House In Virginia."
When he first heard it, he liked to change it up a little and say,

"I have a House In Vietnam, and another one in Venice."

And sometimes, as he rested, or worked, or wrote a new, thinly veiled memory from his distant—or not so distant—past, he thought of those perfect twins from his boyhood, how one of them took his own life in a southern state on a military base, how he never heard any details of why the suicide might have occurred, and how they were both so loosely bound by a rarified site somewhere in Virginia.

Acknowledgements

At a poetry festival on Gabriola Island, curated by Hilary Peach, host Jacob Chaos created an anagram for each artist that he introduced. It seemed fitting that well into middle age, I would finally discover that my first name and my surname were so perfectly suited to a jumbled creation of prima-donna-esque proportions.

David Bateman

A Mad Bent Diva

I thank Jacob for this fabulous discovery, and I pay tribute to his life as a wonderful queer artist who assisted me in acknowledging and embracing the diva and the madness within.

Versions of Tampax Tale, Ice, River and Sea, My Mother's Purse, and I Don't Know How To Love were previously published by Frontenac House Press (Calgary) in the following collections of poetry by David Bateman: *'tis pity* (2012), *Designation Youth* (2014)

Special thanks to Aruna Srivastava and Bill Hackborn for an edit that included Bill singing *Secret Love* to Aruna as they went over the manuscript together.

Special thanks to PJ Thomas for her invaluable editing advice and thorough reading of an early version of the manuscript.

Special thanks to Raymond Helkio, for his generosity, his editing, his enthusiastic support with all things queer, and his friendship.

About the Author

David Bateman is an actor, playwright, visual artist, and performance poet currently based in Toronto. His spoken word monologues and solo plays have been presented both nationally and internationally over the past twenty years. He has a PhD from the University of Calgary (English Literature; specialization Creative Writing) and has taught at a variety of Canadian post-secondary institutions including Emily Carr University of Art and Design (Vancouver), Thompson Rivers University (Kamloops), and Trent University (Peterborough). His arts and entertainment reviews have appeared in XTRA, In Toronto, and at: batemanreviews.blogspot.com/